The Murder of Moira Barking

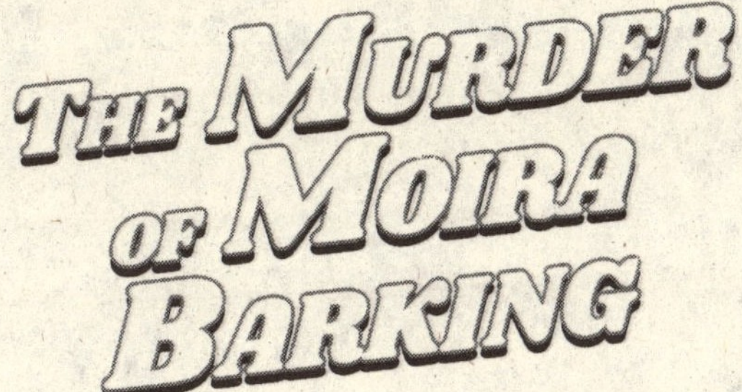

EMILIO COUTINHO SOUSA

Srishti
PUBLISHERS & DISTRIBUTORS

Srishti Publishers & Distributors
A unit of AJR Publishing LLP
212A, Peacock Lane
Shahpur Jat, New Delhi – 110 049

editorial@srishtipublishers.com

First published by Srishti Publishers & Distributors in 2026

10 9 8 7 6 5 4 3 2 1

Printed and bound in India

To Mum and Dad

Part One

Chapter One

It was a rainy February night, and I was sitting in my dorm room, staring at my laptop screen. Colin lay tossing lightly in his bed, occasionally muttering in fits of sleep. Nicholas' bed had been stripped down to the mattress, and his desk, once piled high with books, now sat empty. Outside the window, the night-dark sea spat against the rocks, and the castle grounds were empty and still, save for the flutter of the flag on the northern tower.

It had been a long day already. To start it off, my roommate confessed to murdering his nanny, and then my best friend came along and blew my whole world wide open in the course of a single conversation. Both these rather shocking and inconvenient turns of events sent dozens of moments from the past few months and years tumbling through my mind. Moments that had once seemed meaningless or innocuous had taken on a new, almost sordid meaning.

I tried to sleep, but my thoughts were too loud, and all I would achieve was a sleepless night of tossing and turning. It all started with Regina De Winter. Which, I suppose, wasn't all that surprising; if anyone should blow my world wide open in just a single conversation, it would be her.

She and I had always been telling each other things. She told me that in nursery school, she'd forgotten to close the cage and let out the class rabbit, which resulted in our year being treated to the sight of a crow feasting on the beloved pet; she told me that she spiked the tea in the staff room with laxatives after a slew of particularly bad marks. I, for my part, had told her that in year five, James and I had shared clandestine kisses in the back of Miss Holyrood's class when everyone was gone; I had told her about the time I had taken Grandfather's cufflinks to sell them to a classmate for a bag of sherbet lemons. I'd told her that during a Christmas pageant rehearsal, I was meant to be a shepherd but had loftier ambitions, and so I pushed Charles Pembroke off the stage so I could take his role as the archangel Gabriel. And, I'd told her that in year six, I found Peter Astor sneaking a cigarette behind the chapel. That one paid off well; we blackmailed him into writing our history essays for a term.

Over the years, the pair of us had accumulated, of sorts, a cabinet of secrets, truths, and lies. But, the secret… the secrets we exchanged that night went far deeper than youthful indiscretions and sank into the realms of lies, sin, and murder. She'd come up to me that evening during dinner, and had given me a peck on the cheek and a delicate squeeze of my hand before walking away with Fiona and Polly to Maiden's Tower.

The note she'd subtly tucked into my hand read, 'Library 9:00. Bring no one.'

So, I returned to the dorms and did some homework. Archie, Windsor, and Duffy had joined us for a movie. At around 8:45, I couldn't take it anymore. I left Colin and the others, who were watching Die Hard rather boisterously. I told the on-duty prefect I'd forgotten a textbook in the library and that it couldn't wait because I had an essay due soon. And out I had stepped into the night.

The soft, almost silvery mist had rolled in from the sea, clinging to the grounds, fields, and buildings. I walked down the lamp-lit pathway; a few people walked past me, their laughter and conversation caught in the breeze. I got to the library and slipped in. I went to our usual spot and waited. The only other living thing other than the silverfish was Dottie, the old librarian.

I checked my watch, and it was 8:52. Regina was unlikely to be anything but perfectly punctual. And feeling restless, I got up and paced around. And I found myself in the occult section. The books here, as always, were mostly untouched and sent little puffs of dust into the air when disturbed.

Once, I scoffed at these things as mere superstition, efforts by early man to explain away what he couldn't explain. But now... I was not so sure, and the year has been slow and strange. I remembered that with Baskerville and the whistling of the woods, and him barking away into the trees and shadows. And, I remembered a wild rose on an empty grave. 'There are more things in heaven and earth...'

A hand grasped my shoulder, and I whirled around wildly. Regina De Winter smiled, "My, my, someone is tense." She had changed out of her school uniform into her nightclothes, and her red hair lay across her shoulder in a thick braid.

Regina De Winter was quite the most beautiful person I know; her hair was the colour of red maple in autumn, her skin the colour of Yorkshire snow, and her eyes the blue of summer skies. All in all, she would not be out of place in a pre-Raphaelite painting.

"You're late," I said sulkily. She ignored this. She sank into her usual chair and looked me in the eye for a beat, her gaze boring into me over steepled fingers. "So, darling, how much do you know about the death of Lady Barking?"

I stared at her for a moment before sitting, "Well, not a lot really... just that she's dead. And that it was rather sudden and unexpected. And the date, I suppose," I shrugged,

"And that it was ruled 'unsuspicious'. Do you believe that?" she said, "A woman in her late thirties drops dead, and it's unsuspicious? As ancient as that seems, women in their thirties tend not to drop dead."

Even though we were quite alone, I leaned close and whispered, "Are you saying she was murdered?"

Regina stared distractedly at her fingernails, "Well, Nicky certainly thinks so. And at the very least, her death wasn't down to natural causes."

I watched as she removed a bottle of nail polish from her purse and applied a delicate coat of pink to her nails. "Nicholas believes it to have been murder?"

After a moment, she said, "Hamlet. Three guesses who Nicholas thinks killed his mother." She didn't wait for me to respond before she said, "His father and your mother."

I stared at her, mouth agape.

"Now, I know what you're going to say. 'But, Gina, they couldn't have killed her, neither of them was in London that day!" she said in a rather good imitation of my voice.

She began applying nail polish to her other hand, "And I would say that I think we can both agree that people of their station do not have to deign to anything so pedestrian as to commit murder themselves."

I stared at her, "So, he thinks they paid someone to kill Lady Barking?"

She nodded, 'Yes. But I do not think that to be true. And what's more… I think that woman, Sarah Smith, dying at your mother's Christmas party is connected."

She set down her nail polish. "Now, darling, I am about to tell you something rather shocking… but first…."

It went on. When she was done, I felt as though someone had taken my brain, powdered my thoughts, run them through a sieve, and put them back in. After a moment, Regina smiled sympathetically, "I appreciate that you need a moment, but the library closes soon and lights out at 10:30. And I do have something I need you to do."

"Oh!"

She sighed, "Hamlet, we appear to be reaching the part of the night where you become monosyllabic, and so I shall tell you what indeed you should do. I want you to use that perfect, eidetic memory of yours and write an account of everything that has happened up to this conversation—"

"Everything? Okay, Regina, that's a lot, but I'll be honest, we haven't gone that far back in history class—"

"Hamlet," she said sharply, "You are very droll and very hilarious. But I am quite tired, and so I shall leave you to mull over where it all started for you."

I was about to speak again when she said, "Well, here's where it gets worse."

I sighed, "How can it possibly be worse?"

Regina kicked me under the table, "Well, if you'd let me speak, I could tell you. Well, do you remember what happened after the gargoyle fell? I wouldn't have expected you to notice anything because you were too busy swooning into Jago Keyne's arms—"

"I was not swooning."

"And Colin was too busy sulking about..."

"What does that supposed to mean?"

"But, you see, because I actually pay attention to my surroundings, I did actually notice that something was amiss."

I could tell that she wasn't going to divulge what this mysterious thing was without my pleading and prodding.

"Oh, Regina," I said, trying to sound as sincere as possible. "Please tell me what you noticed. You are ever so intelligent and unappreciated for your genius."

"Okay, darling."

"And you are also so beautiful. And kind too. You put Mother Teresa and Nurse Nightingale..."

"Hamlet, would you just shut up, you petulant prawn!" she said, somehow sounding both heated and still retaining her rather regal way of speaking. "Now, anyway, the thing I noticed was a little stone that fell off the roof."

"I noticed that too, Regina."

"No, you did not."

"Yes. I did it was rather large, shaped like a gargoyle, and nearly took off my head."

I said and almost immediately regretted it.

Regina spoke in a voice of forced cool, "Well, I wasn't talking about the gargoyle. I was talking about a little pebble that fell after the gargoyle fell. Now, what does that little falling pebble tell you?" she asked, arching her eyebrows.

I shrugged, "Gosh. I don't know, Regina. I assume the base of the statue was crumbling."

"You see, I thought that too. But then I realised that that pebble was made of a different material from the gargoyle. It looked like a piece of tile from the roof. Now what does that tell you?" she persisted.

I sighed. "Regina, not that I am not greatly enjoying this guessing game, but can you please just make your point?"

"Fine, Rook. Well, that tells us that someone was on the roof. And that someone pushed the gargoyle onto you," she said, "Don't you see? The killer is targeting you. And I think it's because you saw something… they didn't want you to see. What you saw that night was probably something trivial, something inconspicuous. Something most people wouldn't even notice," she said, "But your mutant brain would have picked up on it, and stored it away. Now, I need you to do what I asked and let me read it on Monday."

I arrived at ten, and the prefect tapped his watch, shooting me a rather disappointed look. Colin was awake, and we talked a lot about a little. I bathed, brushed and now here I sit.

The night is young, and the events of the past several months are whirring fresh in my mind. So, where to begin? I suppose the best place to begin would be when my mother was at the academy or before that even, but that's a bit beyond my patience, much less my scope. But I think I know where to start… and it begins with all things a, seemingly innocuous, gift of flowers….

Chapter Two

24th June, 2023
Rook-Lefey Manor
(near the town of Great Sacrifice, Yorkshire, England)
181 days till the murder of Sarah Smith.

It was the day before my fourteenth birthday, and preparations were ongoing for the summer fete. It was quite chaotic, with a great deal to do in the house with workers setting up fairy lights, tents, buntings and whatnot.

It had been a gorgeous summer, drowsy and dreamy without even a hint of rain. The De Winters and Wendy had come for their usual summer visit. And, on that day, Colin, Regina, Wendy and I were playing a game of cricket on the green and trying to keep well out of the way of the workers.

Mother and Lord Barking had gone to Caithness for a golf tournament, and Grandmother was visiting an old friend, Lady Abernathy-Keith. I had been somewhat in charge of running the house and directing the preparations, which mostly involved relaying Mother's instructions and signing for various items. To be honest, it was getting just a bit wearing, so I was quite glad she was due to return that day.

Anyway, other than that, it was all rather fun until those damned flowers came. Colin had just broken a window, so we weren't surprised to see Flavio the butler shuffling over to us at a very brisk pace.

"Oh shite!" Colin cursed, throwing down his bat and looking very much like a puppy expecting to be kicked, "The penguin's coming."

Colin is tall and stocky, with vibrant ginger hair, freckles, and soulful brown eyes that make it terribly hard for anyone to stay upset at him. The only exception is Flavio, who often finds his workload tripled when the awkward, clumsy Colin is over.

However, as it transpired, Colin needn't have worried because when Flavio got to us, he gave me a rather hurried bow. "Terribly sorry, Lord Hamlet. It's the flowers Her Ladyship ordered for the fete. There appears to have been some sort of mix-up."

I sighed, abandoning my bat and wicket, "Be right back, chums. An heir's work is never done." I followed Flavio over to the front of the house, where a small lorry had parked, and several boxes of flowers were being unloaded. Mother had chosen colourful arrangements bursting with blues, reds and violets, but what was delivered were several large bouquets of white flowers that almost reached my knees. There were definitely no whites in the arrangements Mother had ordered. Nevertheless, I signed for the delivery. I then noticed a little card with my name attached to the white bouquet.

It was a deep green, and on the front in delicate handwriting was my name and, on the back (On the little sticky flap bit that you have to lick and then stick to the lower part of the envelope, which, according to a rather pointless flip through a dictionary, is called a seal flap), was a crest of arms. Most of my friends' families have at least one, but I could not recognize this one for the life of me; a man's face shrouded by vines and shrubbery.

Regina had strolled down the garden path, "I got terribly warm, and the sun is far too bright for my complexion. I shall need my umbrella."

"Do you recognise this coat of arms?" I asked.

Regina took it with a slight frown, "No… I don't," she said, "but you could probably find the answer inside that envelope."

"Right," I said. As it transpired, Regina was dead wrong; opening that envelope only raised more questions. I tore it open and pulled out the glossy, creamy card.

> *To my Darling Hammy. I hope you're having a marvellous birthday. I can't wait to meet you.*
> *—Your loving aunt*

Regina's frown deepened by an inch, "No name… how very rude."

I shrugged, shoving the card away into my pocket. "Probably a long-lost great aunt. I'll ask my mother later. Anyway, Flavio, Mother wants half the arrangements as centre pieces for the tables in the tea garden. The rest are to be used on the archway for the new hedge maze. Will you give the instructions to the decorators?"

Flavio bowed, "Yes, My Lord."

Regina frowned down at the white flowers, "What kind of flowers are they?"

I shrugged, looking at the flowers, "Zinnias, I think.... anyway, I am positively famished. Time for lunch, I think."

Colin, Wendy, Regina, and I sat down to a lunch of wild mushroom soup, roast chicken, and summer pudding. Mother and Lord Barking had called to say they would be back within the hour and had apparently won their tournament.

You know, I've always found golf terribly boring, but well, Mother, Lord Barking and all their friends think of it as the king of sports and won't hear a word against it, so I've learned to hold my tongue, on that matter at least.

Colin and Wendy were talking about calf raises or something of the sort, and Regina and I were talking about the St James family. "Well, we went to that spinning restaurant," I was saying, "You know the one by the Thames?

"Oh, you mean The Ambassador? Well, what did you have and what did you and James talk about?" she asked

"Well, I ordered the chicken. It was rather dry, though. And we talked about football... well, he called it soccer."

"See," Colin interjected between mouthfuls of pudding, "I told you he was no good. Who on earth calls it soccer?"

Regina ignored him, "Do go on, darling."

I nodded, "Yes. And well, my mother and his dad were there, and all they talked about was Second Eden. And the exploration launch. It's very interesting, I suppose."

"Hello, hello," came Mother's voice suddenly. She and Lord Barking had strolled in, both with broad smiles and sun-kissed faces.

"Oh, hello Mum, how was the tournament?" I said, and there was a chorus of 'hellos' as she dropped into her seat.

"It was gorgeous weather, and we won! I do think some of my clubs need refurbishing," she said, pouring herself some wine. "Anyway, have any of the windows suffered any casualties?"

Colin chuckled nervously, "Well, maybe one or two."

Lord Barking slapped my shoulder, his artificial leg whirring and clanking as he shifted his weight and took the seat across from Mother, "I dare say your mother was half afraid you'd burn the place down. Isn't that right, Izzy?"

A lot of people seem to dislike Lord Barking. They all call him the 'spider' or 'the spin doctor'. But I have always been rather fond of him. He might be a spider, but he's a rather jolly, jovial spider. He's a tall man, rather pale, with inky black hair and blue eyes. He'd lost a leg when he was younger, but I am not quite sure how.

"Nonsense," my mother had said while sipping her wine, "I had absolute faith in you, sweetheart. Or at least faith that Wendy would douse any fires – metaphorical or otherwise."

I gave a faux offended gasp, and Wendy smiled, "I did try, Godmother, but the three of them just do not listen."

"Oh, hush," I said, and she stuck her tongue out at me.

"Lord Barking, will Electra be attending the fete tomorrow?" I asked, "I haven't seen her since January. I have so many questions about the polo team and about the Academy."

"Not to mention," Regina interjected, "Electra and I have a score to settle. She and I came to a draw in our last shooting competition, and I am terribly looking forward to breaking it."

"Oh, I am afraid you will have to wait a bit longer. Moira has an appointment or something of the sort tomorrow and wants Electra to be there with her.

"Oh dear," said Wendy, "Is Her Grace ill?"

Lord Barking shrugged, "I shouldn't think so, she seemed quite well when I left. I imagine it's a hair appointment or something like that."

Mother spoke, "You know, Harry, I was thinking. Why not bring Nicholas up here? He might enjoy the fresh air… and the company."

Nicholas Barking being in my house and ruining my summer was quite possibly the closest thing to hell on earth I could imagine, and I was about to protest, but luckily Lord Barking sighed deeply as he always did when reminded of Nicholas' existence, "Nicholas is Nicholas. The boy never takes his nose out of his books. Not to mention that he dislikes the outdoors, crowds, the sun, and the rain. I am sure he'd be much happier in London with his books and Moira fussing over him constantly. Besides, she's taking him to some play they've both been going on about."

"Which play?" Wendy asked, for some reason wanting to prolong this conversation.

"Midsummer Night's Dream, I believe. Although I would have preferred Richard III."

Mother frowned; she'd always had great sympathy for Nicholas, and had been about to say something when Flavio had come bustling into the room looking rather harried. "Lady Isohel, Your Grace, Lord Hamlet…" he said, punctuating each name with a bow at the respective person.

Flavio never gives much away, and his usual demeanour (at least with me) is one of indignation, so none of us could guess what news he had for us. "There is a call from Cimmerian Manor. They say they have been trying to reach His Grace all morning."

Lord Barking sighed, "I expect it's the usual trivial inconvenience blown out of proportion. I suppose I should see what it is."

Mother waved him down, "Don't worry, darling. Hamlet will get it." I nodded, dabbing at my lips with my napkin and went over to Mother's office. I picked up the receiver, "Hello?"

There was a moment of dead silence before a female voice came across at the end, "Where's my father?" Electra Barking's voice was sharp, fragile, almost keening.

"Electra," I said as gooseflesh prickled up my skin. "Has something happened?"

Her voice was tremulous, and a cacophony of voices filled the background. "Where is my father? He hasn't answered his phone all morning…Where is he?"

I swallowed, "Electra… he and my mother were at the golf tournament in Dunnet Head. They just got back."

Electra's laugh was like the tinkling of shattered glass, "Well, do me a favour. Tell him his wife died this morning." And the line went dead.

I walk-d slowly back to the dining room. There was the lilt of laughter and easy conversation; Colin was telling a funny story.

You know, in the movies, when someone receives bad news, they're always quite quiet and calm about it. Their faces go blank, they stutter, and sink into a chair. But in my experience, grief is quite loud. Mother wailed when Grandfather died, and Lord Barking screamed in rage when I told him about Lady Barking. The conversation died, and Lord Barking's face changed colour several times before settling on an angry red. With a cry of anger that stung the ears, he leapt to his feet and walked right out of the room without another word. Mother's face was blank, and all the colour drained from it. Her eyes, green like mine, danced around the room, staring at nothing, as though each shadow contained a hundred different nettlesome problems. After a moment, she followed him.

Out on the moor, dark, grey clouds bruised out the sun. And on the wind, there was a crackle of thunder and the smell of rain.

Chapter Three

Outside, a summer storm kissed the trees and windowpanes, darkening the sun. The days so far had been long and golden with only the rarest of showers. And, even with the Michaelmas term fast approaching, there were only the softest murmurs of autumn.

That is, until that day. The rain broke that day – a dark, bruised-looking sky with the low rumble of thunder. We found ourselves playing board games and card games to pass the time.

Granny, who grew up in Goa and acquired a taste for antique Portuguese furniture, had decorated that room in blues and whites. It was one of my favourite parts of the house. If I had to give it a definite ranking, it would be fourth, after my bedroom, the sunroom, and the glass mahal.

It's a rather lovely old room, with carved furniture and large French windows that opened directly into the garden. (Of course, one is not supposed to come in through the French windows even though it would be incredibly convenient, as Mother doesn't want mud in the house.)

And it is there we sat, as the rain pattered against the windows, turning the moor and gardens a silver grey. Flavio had set the bouquet of white zinnias on the centre table; Now indoors, I could faintly smell them – they had a queer, floral and slightly bitter aroma to them.

Well, anyway, before we proceed, there was one important thing to know about Nicholas Barking, and it is that he was simply the worst. And his mother, Moira Barking, the now late Duchess of London, was by far the most unpleasant woman I have ever met and the bane of my childhood. Nicholas would pick fights with me in school. And when I fought back, we invariably got in trouble because she would swoop in to his defence, going on and on about how Nicholas was an angel and I was a wicked, spoiled child overindulged by my mother. And of course, the irony was utterly lost on her. So, as one can imagine, I didn't exactly mourn her passing. I put on a polite face of sadness, but internally I was humming the chorus to 'Ding Dong the witch is dead'.

I had been one card away from getting UNO when Coin had slapped me with a plus four. "You are picking on me, aren't you?" I said, "Anyway, it is sad about Lady Barking," I continued, "But I don't see why we have to go to the funeral."

Wendy frowned at me, "To support poor Nick and Electra. They are your friends."

"Well, Electra is," I muttered.

Regina shrugged, "Well, going is the right thing and what's expected. But I do doubt Lady Barking would want us there... She wasn't too fond of us."

"Remember at Duffy's sixth birthday party? Nicholas pulled my hair, and so I shoved him. And then Lady Barking slapped me."

Wendy began tentatively, "Well, you did push her son—"
"In a sandbox, Wends, not down a cliff."

"Given that what might be an everyday tumble for another child might be fatal for her son," she said sharply. "You can forgive her for hovering and for being upset you almost sent her son to the hospital with a nosebleed."

Oh yes," Colin said, "I forgot he's… what's the word?'

"Haemophiliac," Regina provided.

I wanted to point out that he wasn't the only haemophiliac in the world, simply the most unpleasant, but I held my tongue because I'm polite.

"Indeed," Wendy had said, "Nicholas has haemophilia, which is why he can't play sports. So, you will have to forgive Lady Barking for being upset that you pushed her son."

"Again," I said, "He started it."

"Hamlet, that doesn't matter," Wendy started, "You need to control your temper. And not to mention you shoved Lady Barking into the pool!"

I couldn't help but chuckle, "Oh come on. That was only after she slapped me, besides Mother grounded me for a week… besides, Wendy…" I said, interrupting the impending lecture, "What else was I supposed to do? Turn the other cheek?"

"You could have told—"

"Told whom? The mother?"

She stuttered for a moment. "Well, you could have told a parent or an adult."

Colin frowned, "Well, that never really did any good, did it? Anytime anyone tried to discipline him, Lady Barking would descend and whisk him away."

"But, you're right, I do feel for Nicholas," I added, "He was ever such a mother's boy."

Regina made a delicate sort of snorting sound, "You're one to talk!"

Wendy protested, "You two really shouldn't be joking about this awful matter."

"Oh, come on, Wends," I said, "we're making fun of Nicholas, not poor Lady Barking."

Regina stared at her cards and said rather bored, "I, for one, think he's dreadfully handsome, a cross between Alain Delon and Jane Birkin. That dark hair, and those brooding bluish grey eyes…"

I didn't know who those people were." I, for one, thought Nicholas Barking looked like the Grim Reaper, but I did not argue.

"It's just so terrible," Wendy said, for what must have been the fifth time. "Just such a tragedy. "She wasn't even sick, was she?"

Regina frowned at her cards, "You know. That is just what I was thinking. We saw her on the sports day, and she was fine. And that was two months ago. But then we saw her at the St Brelade's regatta two weeks ago, and she seemed fine."

"Yes, she did," I said. I could still remember seeing the old witch, with her perfectly manicured hands and perfectly coiffed hair. I had been sitting with the De Winters, watching the races, and she had walked behind us holding a mimosa. She had not looked like a woman who would drop dead out of the blue.

Lady Barking, all things considered, was an extraordinarily spry woman. Every morning on the way to school, I'd see her doing her daily jog, rain or shine. She also competed in marathons, Ironman events, and the like.

"It's just so shocking," Wendy said again, now sounding close to tears, "She was such a… lively (overzealous) woman. Always involved with the PTA (excessively) and with the school (obsessively). I can't imagine what Nick and Lexie are going through."

I rolled my eyes. Wendy certainly seemed distraught, but I just felt a bit annoyed. 'Lively' was one word for it. As far as I could remember, I hadn't thought she really cared about anything other than making her children look good.

"Oh, maybe she was bumped off," Colin said, dropping his last card onto the pile, causing Wendy to gasp. rather dramatically

Regina cut across her, "If so, we don't know the how... and the who... if there is a who?"

I looked up at her, "Aren't they both obvious?" Regina frowned at me, and I went on, "Who was a farm girl from Kansas, and the how was a bucket of water."

Regina rolled her eyes at this.

Wendy seemed about to gasp yet again, but just then Colin got bored with Uno and said, "Is it poor taste to suggest we play Cluedo?"

I don't know whether it was in poor taste, but we did end up playing Cluedo. Colin spoke, "You know, Hammy, you should text Electra. You used to have a massive crush on her, remember? This is your way in."

"Now, now, Colin," I said scoldingly, "That would hardly be proper."

Just then, the door to the drawing room swung open, and Mother poked her head in, still wearing her golf whites. Her face was pale, with a sort of drawn quality. She seemed to have aged ten years in the last two hours. "Just thought I ought to let you know the fete has been called off," she said in a quiet voice. "It just wouldn't be appropriate."

"Cancelled what?" I asked. My voice came out sharper than I intended, and I felt my face get very hot. "It's… it's tomorrow. Everything's ready. It's my birthday; you can't just cancel it."

She sighed shakily, "Darling, it would not be appropriate—"

"And…" I said, my voice coming out slightly shaky, "Nicholas' mother being dead is an appropriate reason to make me cancel my birthday party?"

She did not respond; she was staring past me. I thought for a moment that something was outside the window, then realised with an odd pang that it was the white bouquet she was staring at. And something in her face shifted. It wasn't anger precisely… or rather, it wasn't anger alone. She looked almost as though someone had walked over her grave. And after a moment of silence, she said in a voice of quiet fear. Anger? Both?

"Where did these flowers come from?"

"They came from Fionnula's, as always… came with a card," I stared at her, feeling some of my annoyance and irritation melt away. I was not in the mood to deal with anything else, but I couldn't help but feel a little bit worried about her. I had never seen her look... well, not lost, but shaken, perhaps.

I handed her the note, "It says it's from my aunt… who could it be? I don't really have any aunts other than on dad's side, but—"

"*Shush*!" Mother snapped her voice into a sharp hiss, and her eyes darted around the room, taking in the flowers again and again, and her face grew ever redder. "The funeral shall be held tomorrow. I think you all had better start packing. We shall be returning to London early."

My mother has never spoken to me like that before. Never in my life had I ever been silenced. Even as a child, I could walk into her board meetings whenever I pleased, demanding whatever took my fancy, whether it be stories or toys or whatever, she'd only laugh, ignoring the muttered protest and take me onto her lap. Even grandpa used to let me sit on his lap during cabinet meetings. So, needless to say, I was rather shaken, and I felt myself getting angry. But Mother left before I could say anything.

Regina watched Mother slip out the door and close it behind her. She then turned to me, looking as utterly bemused as I felt, and said, "I guess your mother does not like zinnias very much."

"I guess not."

Chapter Four

The rain, gentle now, carried the scent of heather and ozone across the moors, a fleeting reprieve for those inclined to romanticize bleak landscapes and their inconvenient weather. When the last cup was drained, Regina and I led Baskerville into the cooling dusk, heading toward Whistling Woods. Along the path, festival detritus accumulated: bunting stowed, tents collapsing, voices dissolving into the gathering gloom of twilight.

"A shame about the fête," Regina remarked, the sort of understated eulogy one expects at country gatherings derailed by sudden death. My own ill feelings lay in the unjust cancellation of my birthday plans, and I had a suspicion that the old witch had died out of spite for me.

Lady Barking, if we're generous, was a woman better avoided. If one is feeling less charitable, she might be described as a spite-motivated harpy of a woman, and her demise both inconvenient and oddly theatrical.

"Everything is stupid and annoying," I muttered, "I hate this weather, I hate the stupid fete, I hate Lady Barking for dying and ruining everything."

"Yes, yes," Regina said coolly. "Don't we all."

Baskerville, undeterred by human drama, chased after a stick; the woods, meanwhile, seemed at once refuge and foreboding threshold. "Poor Lady Barking," we said, mostly to fill the silence.

We walked for a few moments before Regina, out of the blue, requested the note received with the flowers, a curious emblem with a crest I could not place, despite my grandfather teaching me all about heraldry, making me memorise all the crests of every noble family in the country. The note itself, the handwriting, the peculiar greeting, "I simply can't wait to meet you," struck Regina as noteworthy, the choice of 'meet' for a circle where 'see you' would be customary. As she pointed out, the letter was otherwise rather familiar, what with calling me 'Hammy' and all that. I'll be honest, I didn't think much about it. People make all sorts of mistakes when writing or typing. Grammar is a fickle mistress after all.

But, Mother had been so deeply unsettled by the flowers, a fact Regina read as something more than her usual obsessive fussiness, but just what else Regina wasn't sure yet.

We continued, arm in arm, the woods closing around us. It was an old-growth woodland, and I believe the last remaining forest in all of England that dated back to that unknown period before history began. The trees were pedunculate oak, rowan, holly, and yew. The wind whistled and called as it danced through them. This was, of course, why the woods are called 'the Whistling Woods', and there is a rather long-winded scientific explanation of the topography and tree placement. But as a child, I had often thought I saw a man standing here or there, and once he was so close, I could have touched him. And I could have sworn he was the one whistling, trying to lure me away.

It is in these woods that I spent most of my childhood. In the early days, before I started school, my only playmates were the trees, and Baskerville and the stuffed dragon Granny had knitted for me. And after I'd met Regina and Colin and the lads, we'd go to each other's houses or whatnot, I still longed for these woods. And when they'd visit in summer or long weekends, we'd spend all day in the woods playing at pretend kingdoms.

As we walked, Regina wrapped her arms around mine. "Funerals and flowers," she said, "I can't help but feel like something is afoot."

I couldn't help but raise my eyebrows at that, "Afoot? Seriously, that's your choice of words?"

She rolled her eyes and ignored that, "Well, we shall see, I suppose."

We realised we'd wandered farther than intended, but the odd thing was that we were walking towards the fairy lights; we ended up away from the house rather than towards it.

Chapter Five

The day's strangeness was everywhere, pressing against the quiet rhythms of a house unsettled and unmoored. Mother, overwrought, skipped dinner. Flavio, uncomplaining and diligent, left her a plate outside the door, later retrieving it, untouched, cold. Granny, mercifully returned before nightfall, handed her coat to Flavio with the calm efficiency born of decades in drafty English houses. "She's still in her room, I suppose?"

"Oh yes. She took Lady Barking's death to heart."

Granny's smile, faint and knowing, signalled neither agreement nor surprise. The emotional logic of country houses, after all, is a peculiar thing.

Ignoring warnings not to disturb, Granny advanced upon Mother's room, refusing the typical rituals of privacy. "Sit up. I brought you dinner."

The curtains were drawn tight, but ritual prevailed. Mother shifted to the vanity, toyed with her food. "What's this about attending tomorrow's funeral?"

"It's expected."

Granny responded sharply: "Expected, yes, but not necessarily appropriate."

In the gloom, Mother strained to keep her composure, exhaustion etched deep mingled with what looked like guilt "Harry wants me there. I can't abandon him."

Later, I exiled myself to my room, which is quite possibly, if not most definitely, my favourite place in all creation. Every swish of fabric from the curtains to the linen, to the upholstery on the twin armchairs, to the window seats is a delightful shade of green, the precise shade of green of a mallard's feathers. And then, of course, the windows looked out at the moor and forest, large and ornate, an ancestor's protest against a window tax.

But even there, I couldn't find peace, much less sleep, as my discontent thickened as did my confusion. 'Aunt'. The card had said. But I have no aunts, not that Mother was an only child. She had a sister who died in childhood. My father, whom I haven't seen since I can remember, might have had brothers and sisters, but I doubt any of them would take any more interest in me than he did.

Nor was that the only thing rattling around my head; I couldn't stop thinking about Lady Barking. The more I thought about it, the more unnatural it felt that she was dead. She was such a steady figure; it seemed quite odd that she might be suddenly gone.

Regina arrived with irrepressible energy, landing on the bed. "Guess what? Zinnias are a message from an absent friend." But before I could respond, I noticed something.

A sudden flicker outside the window caught my eye. A figure walked alone through the rain, holding a lantern aloft. I stared at the figure as it walked away from the house down the garden.

"Regina," I whispered, and in a flash, she was by my side. We watched the figure walking somewhat unsteadily down the garden path and stepping into the Old Yew Alley.

"How nosy are we feeling?" asked Regina. The answer arrived in sodden shoes and a hurricane lamp, and we followed Granny's path past the greenhouse and through rain-kissed gardens, ripe with jasmine and lavender.

Out on Rook Moor, under the moon's silver spotlight, only Jack's Tor stood removed from light, a jagged presence we hurried past. And, Regina glowed, spectral and luminous, white nightgown trailing. "The family crypt is that way," I whispered, sudden understanding dull but insistent.

Granny pressed on, lamp casting her as something from half-remembered tales, kneeling finally among gravestones in a ritual of grief. The elm tree stood sentinel, watching as Granny walked on, unwavering, straight and purposeful, with her lamp held aloft. Soon the mausoleum swelled out of the darkness, and Granny unlocked the lychgate and picked her way through the gravestones, ignoring them all, until finally she paused for a moment at one, lowering herself to her knees in the wet earth. We did not disturb her, but once she'd passed, we slipped forth into the graveyard. The stones, silent and shining in the rain, stood undisturbed, save for one with a flower on its base. The grave belongs to my mother's late sister. Lady Dahlia Rook's grave. "Your aunt," Regina whispered.

We looked at each other for a beat, and then the lamp guttered. A face, or only its absence, flickered in the mausoleum window. Rain and childhood shadows conspired, returning us indoors: children, even now, jumping at ghosts.

Chapter Six

25th June, 2023
Cathedral of St Benedicta,
The Rolling Rocks, London
180 days till the murder

Is there anything drearier than a London funeral? The city never felt like home to me – too cramped, too confining, a place where endless crowds steal one's breath. My happiest memories belong to the manor, vast and wild, where summers unfolded in golden light, and winters whispered in the crackling fireplace. For the first five years of my life, the manor was my universe, Baskerville and my stuffed dragon, days illuminated by sun and glow worms, evenings rounded by stories on Grandpa's knees.

I was a wilful child, squalling all the way to the city, wriggling free only after Mother and the driver pried me out. It was then that I met Regina, who took my unchecked wails with an elegant disdain that would become her hallmark. At those pastel desks in kindergarten, beside Colin and Archie, I found my place amid the city's crowd, but Rook Manor has felt more like home, more than London's grey streets ever had.

Saint Benedicta's Cathedral, technically the Cathedral of St Benedicta of The Rolling Rock sits in one of London's older parts; it's a large structure in a large field of green and tombstones. But today it seemed to float, ghostlike, behind a veil of relentless rain and fog. The spires and buttresses seemed almost like spectral hands grasping the sky.

Our carriage slowed before the cathedral, where a small swarm of camera-bearing figures buzzed about. "Are they all here for the funeral?" Colin murmured.

"Given the Barkings' influence," Regina replied, her umbrella blooming as we stepped onto slick cobblestones, "one would expect nothing less. Lady Barking's sudden death has certainly turned heads."

Inside, Lord Barking and his children, Nicholas and Electra, greeted mourners with the patent unsettling Barking grace. They looked very much alike; all tall, slender figures with jet-black hair, marble-pale skin, and icy blue eyes. They are an attractive family, I suppose, but on that day, with their sunken, drawn faces and tired eyes, they all looked rather like the walking dead.

Lord Barking seemed to see only Mother, walking right past me to embrace her for a long moment that drew a few sideways glances. When they parted, Mother avoided his gaze, murmured condolences, and melted into the pews.

Nicholas stood motionless, eyes icy, studying my mother and his father with an odd intensity. I offered a handshake; after a moment of silence, he took it. He and his mother were very close. Poor thing must have felt like the world was pulled out from under him.

Electra, of course, was more polite, and even in grief, she was ethereal in her beauty. She took my hand, nodded her thanks, and I stepped away.

The coffin sat heavily before the altar. Lady Barking lay in state, her lace gloves clutching a silver rosary, her face veiled. For a fleeting moment, she seemed almost to rise, shedding the veil with that familiar sneer. But mercifully, she remained quite dead.

Regina, beside me, gave a respectful bow. Together, we approached Mother, seated alone, distant from the crowd. Her gloved hands fidgeted restlessly with the black cloth of her dress; her eyes darted skyward, as if the angels and saints in their glass precipices were watching her, judging her.

I had drifted off studying the stone and glass faces above 'The Sleeping Court', forgotten queens and princes and dragons frozen amid a dance of swords and spinning wheels. Their stories were vague, lost in time and myth, and there are only a few who remember them.

Then Regina's gloved hand closed around my wrist. Whispers floated over us as passersby cast furtive glances toward Mother. But she, impassive as a marble statue, ignored them all.

Sir Tom Keyne and his wife settled behind Mother. Lady Keyne's hand reached forward, resting lightly on Mother's shoulder, her voice a tender murmur: "Isohel, everyone's fussing over Harry. I just wanted to see how you're holding up."

Mother's eyes remained fixed. Something flashed across her face, a momentary crack so sour, so hate-filled that it could curdle milk before Lady Keyne withdrew.

"That was rude," I whispered, "Lady Kenye was—"

Mother's sidelong glance carried all the warning of a suddenly retreating tide, so I shut up.

Fr John took the altar, the choir sang 'Abide with Me', and the priest read from the Gospel of John about Lazarus's resurrection. The mass proceeded in a solemn, sacred decorum until the second reading, delivered by none other than Nicholas:

"Beloved, leave room for the wrath of righteousness; for vengeance is mine, I will repay. If your enemies' hunger, feed them; if they thirst, give them drink, for heaping burning coals on their heads."

Regina's whisper cut through my thoughts. "I don't think that's the assigned reading."

Fr John's brow furrowed; Lord Barking's was a pale mask of fury simmering beneath restraint. It certainly was a violent verse, a bit out of place, but I doubt Nicholas, as stupid as he was, was idiotic enough to make a scene at his own mother's funeral.

As Nicholas returned to his seat, Lord Barking's clenched jaw tightened, but he said nothing. The Mass resumed without further incident. And we followed the coffin from the cathedral to the churchyard, where two stone angels stood vigil, their rain-washed faces seeming to weep.

The priest's hands extended over the dark wood, invoking resurrection and eternity. Electra's eulogy was poised and heartfelt; Lord Barking remained stoic and mute.

And then, to general surprise, Mother walked with purpose up to the graveside and spoke rather quickly about being friends with Lady Barking at the academy and reciting, "Do not stand at my grave and weep." She then joined Lord Barking, where he stood.

The choir's 'Nearer My God to Thee' filled the cold air as the coffin sank beneath the earth. One by one, we approached to cast handfuls of soil onto the casket.

Electra's steady gaze never wavered from the void where mother was. Nicholas, however, watched Mother intently as she completed the ritual, crossing herself before returning to Lord Barking.

I scattered earth onto the grave, attempting to summon a kind thought; if nothing else, Lady Moira had been energetic, and surely raising Nicholas was no easy feat. "Rest in peace," I murmured.

"What an odd funeral," Regina remarked behind me.

"How so?" I asked, eyes fixed on the lone ash tree.

"Lord Barking's silence, Nicholas's heavy-handed reading on vengeance…"

We drifted among tombstones. "Did you notice? There was a veil, some covering, over her face."

Interlacing our fingers, Regina smiled. "Sudden deaths tend to leave one… unprepared."

I frowned. "Then why an open coffin?"

"To make a point," she said coolly. "Everything staged, the silence, your mother's poem. A performance."

"What point?"

"That Lord Barking has nothing to hide," her eyes sharp.

"But isn't that precisely why one hides something?"

Our fingers brushed the ancient ash tree. Ashes live a millennium or more, long predating London and Christianity itself.

A twig snapped, and we turned sharply to find a woman near, cigarette and lighter in hand.

"Sorry," she said sheepishly. "Needed a smoke break."

Regina offered a sweet smile. "No harm done."

The woman, Delilah Keyne, wife of Sir Tom, exuded effortless charm: raven hair, warm brown eyes, coffee-colored skin.

"Poor Moira," she mused, sighing, lighting her cigarette. "So sudden, so tragic. People whisper – accident, suicide. She adored those children, especially the boy. I don't believe she left willingly."

Regina studied her closely. "You never truly know anyone."

Delilah smiled knowingly. "And you'd do well to remember that."

We parted ways, promising to meet again.

"I expect we will," Delilah said, "I'm deputy headmistress at the academy."

Regina's grip tightened on my elbow. "Hamlet," she said, nodding toward the grave, wreathed with roses, lilies, and a massive bouquet of white dahlias.

"There are secrets, Hammy," she whispered. "And you and I are far too curious not to unearth them."

I nodded with resolve. "Indeed, we shall."

Chapter Seven

London, August 2023
5 months till the murder

Not much of note happened in the days after the funeral. At school, Lady Barking's death was cause for loads of morbid gossip as there was a great deal of secrecy surrounding her death. We surmised that the veil was because she'd died in a particularly gruesome manner. We'd all become armchair detectives and amateur psychotherapists trying to figure out what exactly had happened. Some suggested she'd fallen down a particularly long flight of stairs or got into a car crash. One even suggested poison. Then someone suggested the possibility of suicide, and hence all the secrecy. Regina, however, half smiled, "Well, that or she was murdered."

And there followed a great deal of laughter, but Regina didn't join in. And neither did I.

After school one day, Regina and I were taking Baskerville for a walk. Even on pleasant days, walking in London or, I suppose, any city is such an unfriendly and almost nerve-wracking experience; one must duck and weave around scores of people, and more than anything else, the endless traffic. But there is Old Bridge Park, which is one of my favourite places in London. It's rather close to the house and sits right on the river.

As we walked together, Regina was silent. The thing about Regina De Winter is that she's only silent when she's cross or contemplative. And as I was very sure I'd done nothing (at least on that day) to earn her ire, I looked at her, "Everything quite all right, darling?"

She seemed for a moment like one roused from a dream. "Oh, nothing, my apologies if I am not good company today."

I decided not to prod and to just wait until she was ready to tell me what was on her mind. We strolled in silence around the park and bumped into none other than Electra Barking. "Oh, hello, Electra," Regina said in a tone of polite and pleasant surprise,

Electra looked as tired and pale as she was on the day of the funeral, but she smiled, "Oh, hello, Regina… Hamlet."

I smiled up at Electra, "And where are you off to on this fine autumn afternoon?"

"Oh, I am just on my way to school," she said. "Father wants me to pick up some paperwork. Something about Nicholas and home-schooling."

"Oh, dear me... home-schooling? Well, I do suppose parents know best," Regina said.

Electra's smile was almost sardonic, "One would think." And then after a beat, "Terribly sorry, but I really should hurry, the office closes soon," she said, stepping past us.

Regina turned as she did, "Do you think it would be alright if Hamlet and I called in on your dad?"

Electra nodded, "Oh, yes. Do go on. I am sure he would be glad of the company."

"Poor thing," I mused as we watched Electra's retreating back, "I almost don't recognise her."

"Why on earth would you want to visit Barking?" I asked.

And Regina tutted, "Oh, just a compassionate visit. Poor things must be getting so very lonely. Poor Nicholas has missed quite a bit. It's only right that we go and inform him of any assignments he might have missed. It would be a terrible shame if he were to have to repeat the year."

I sighed, "Fine. I am only coming along to see Lord Barking, but I shan't be staying more than fifteen minutes."

She sighed a De Winter sigh, "Oh, darling, don't be dramatic. The poor boy just lost his mother. He would no doubt appreciate friendly faces such as ours."

"Yes," I said, "Because our presence would no doubt ease Nicholas in his grief. He is so very fond of us."

"Oh, don't be naïve, darling," she said now, a touch impatient, "I am not suggesting it will bring him comfort. We are going to satisfy our curiosity. We do have a secret to crack."

And together we walked through the park and out towards the Barking house. It was officially called Cimmerian Manor or The Thamesgate, but we called it the Kennel (because of the barking dogs). It sat on the other side of the park and was practically built into the river. Regina lifted the large knocker, shaped like a dog, and let it fall once, then twice.

After a beat or two, Nicholas opened the door, positively glowering, "What do you people want?" he said in a snarl. Regina ignored my pointed look and gave a soft, simpering laugh, "Now, darling, that is no way to greet guests, especially not old friends."

Nicholas' pale eyes bored holes into her skull. "Why are you here, De Winter?"

She gave him a coy smile, "Oh, because, darling, we just wanted to see how you are doing. We are all worried about you."

Nicholas' cold eyes bore into her face, "Well, I am doing quite all right. You may leave now." His father appeared over his shoulder, "Now, now, son, remember yourself. Do invite our guests in."

Nicholas didn't even look at his father, but with a sigh, he sidestepped, "Fine. But the bloody beast stays outside," he said, jabbing a pale finger at Baskerville. Lord Barking chuckled, "Nonsense. This handsome old man is welcome too."

Baskerville, for his part, was absolutely overjoyed to see Lord Barking, and he wagged his tail and patted his feet about in almost puppy-like excitement. Lord Barking led us inside the house, and I was filled with an impression of greys and blacks. Where Rook Manor is all warm colours and sunlight, it seemed the Barkings preferred a rather muted colour palette.

He led us into a drawing room that overlooked the silver streak of the Thames, and we seated ourselves on high-backed chairs. Regina simpered, Baskerville wagged his tail, and Nicholas glowered. "How's your mother doing?" Lord Barking asked, and Baskerville sat at his feet, his big, floppy black head resting on his knee while Lord Barking petted him.

"Oh, um… well, she's doing quite well. Thank you. She's busy with work and the like," I said. Regina leaned forward, "How are you doing, Your Grace?"

Lord Barking sighed, "Well, as you can imagine. It's been a tricky few weeks."

"And, Nicholas, how are you?" Regina pressed on. "We were worried you would miss out on schoolwork, so we came to catch you up."

Lord Barking smiled, "Terribly kind of you both. But nothing to worry about on that score. We have hired a home-school tutor."

He called out, and a few moments later, a blond-haired woman walked down the stairs and entered the drawing room.

"This wonderful young woman…" Lord Barking said, "…is Miss Sarah Smith… this is Lord Hamlet Rook-Lefey, And Lady Regina De Winter."

Miss Smith held out a hand. She had brown eyes and a warm smile. "Pleased to meet you both."

We shook her hand and Regina held on for a fraction of a second longer than strictly necessary. "So you work for the school?"

Nicholas interrupted, "My mum hired her. Mother said an old friend recommended her. She works for an agency recommended by the school. They provided her with the syllabus and the requisite material."

For the first time in all the time I've known him, Nicholas Barking seemed flustered. There was something very odd here. Very odd indeed. Regina shot a sideways glance at me, our eyes meeting for a moment.

"Oh, really?" Regina said, "So I do take it that you're all caught up then? In history, we're studying the Napoleonic Wars. And in math, we're doing an introduction to algebra."

I was a bit confused because in history we were studying the Gothic Wars, not the Napoleonic Wars, and in math we were in the middle of our geometry segment. But I could tell by the green gleam of her eyes she was up to something (as always).

Nicholas nodded, his eyes dancing around the room, "Yes, of course. She and I just went over the Battle of Waterloo just yesterday. And we watched the movie too. Terribly cracking stuff."

Nicholas is very much not the type to say, 'cracking stuff'. Regina was studying him with the air of a child who'd flipped over a large rock and was poking at whatever slimy thing she'd found beneath. Miss Smith nodded. Lord Barking smiled. Nicholas stared at Baskerville. Lord Barking's eyes never left my face, and more than once, he seemed on the verge of wanting to say something but restrained himself.

Miss Smith excused herself, and after some tea, Regina and I made our excuses to leave.

Lord Barking asked me to do him a favour. He disappeared into his office for a few moments, and when he returned, he had a sealed envelope, which he handed to me. "Make sure this gets straight to your mother, son," he said, gripping my shoulder and staring intently at me.

I nodded, "Yes, of course, Lord Harry."

He nodded, satisfied. And then he went back into his office and closed the door.

Nicholas offered to show us out, and then, the second we crossed the threshold into the open, he gripped my arm. "Listen, Rook, you will not breathe a word of this to anyone."

I was rather confused, not knowing exactly what he meant, but I grabbed his wrist and pulled him closer. "Barking, do you recall what happened the last time we fought?"

Regina intervened, slipping an arm around me and pulling me away, "Don't worry, Nicholas, our lips are sealed."

And with that, she and I walked away. "I never liked him," I said as we walked down the street. Regina gave a little sigh, "I know."

"And you do see why… what was that all about anyway? What on earth could be so serious and so secretive that he had to carry on like that?" I rubbed my wrist even though Nicholas' brittle, bony fingers had done little harm.

Regina was silent. We crossed the street and walked back into the park. It was late evening, and it had begun to rain. It was cold autumn rain that made the pavement shine like patent leather. The air grew cool, and the city seemed to slow down.

"We are going to open that envelope, I trust?" she said.

"You have a talent for stating the obvious, Regina. Of course, we're going to open it! But how… I think Mother would notice if the envelope was ripped."

Regina chuckled, "Oh ye of little faith. I have just the thing in my room."

As it transpired, it was a clothes steamer thing. I shouldn't be surprised, as the De Winters are quite a sartorial-minded family. Anyway, she used it to melt the glue. She slid out the note, and together we read:

> *My Darling,*
> *I dare not text or call. Enemies within. Enemies without. Traitors and impostors. I fear an old friend has returned. We all need to be together. We have much to discuss. Write to me at the office.*
>
> *I see you in every sunset,*
> *Your loving Harry.*

Regina studied the note, "Terribly fascinating… a traitor in our midst."

I stared at the note, "Well, what do you suppose we should do?"

Regina gently took the note from my hand, "You do what Lord Barking said and take this straight to your mother." She slid the letter back in and gently, precisely slid a stick of glue across the flap and patted it down.

I took it, "Is that it?"

"Oh, darling, you have a remarkable ability to ask the stupidest questions. Of course, you and I will be investigating."

Mother was sitting by the fireplace, staring into the flames with a cup of tea and a lot of paperwork before her. She didn't react until I was standing right beside her. She looked up, the orange glow of the flames playing on her features, "Oh, hello, love. How was school?"

"The usual. We got the math test back, and I did rather well," I said, not entirely sure how to broach the subject of the letter.

She smiled, "I am not surprised. You did inherit my brains after all."

I couldn't help but laugh despite my unease, "Yes, I daresay I did."

She looked back at her paperwork, and I watched as she worked, scratching her signature into some document or another. "And what did you get up to after school? Did you go down to the Astons' house again?"

"No," I said, "actually, on our way back from school, Regina and I stopped by the Barkings for a compassionate visit."

Mother gave a small smile, "How very sweet. I am sure Harry was happy to see you."

I nodded, "He… he was. And of course, he was happy to see Baskerville."

She smiled fondly, "And how is Harry? And Nicholas?"

"Lord Harry seemed very well. Nicholas is surly as ever. But Lord Harry has taken on a tutor for Nicholas. A home-school tutor," I said.

She curled up an eyebrow, "Oh, really? A tutor?"

I took the letter out of my pocket, "Lord Harry asked that I give you this," I said, handing her the note.

I watched as she took it with a slight frown, slid open the flap and read the note. Her face shifted almost imperceptibly, and then, quietly, she stood, tossed it onto the fire, and watched it burn. "Go do your homework, Hamlet."

I watched the letter blacken and curl. It had been on my tongue to ask about the imposter and the traitor, but she probably wouldn't react well to my prying. And so, I merely nodded and walked up the stairs and into my room.

Chapter Eight

London
31st October, 2023

The months that followed drifted by with the lethargy of a London fog, and the Barkings mercifully disappeared from my world for several months. The football finals loomed (which we did win, but victory was bittersweet cause the heel on my favourite studs wore out) and the approach of the Academy filled us all with a sort of restless anticipation. School life had neatly partitioned us: Wendy nested with her ballet cohort, while Regina, Colin, and I nested with Archie Aston, Duffy St Brelade, Prince Windsor of Wales, my teammates and Fiona Kingsley and Polly Shrewsbury, who graced the field hockey side alongside Regina. We dubbed ourselves 'The Darlings', most ironic, I think.

By late October, the cold had set in. One bleak afternoon, Regina and I walked Baskerville through Old Bridge Park. The river, the sky, the trees – all a monochrome wash of muted greys, but Baskerville, undeterred, went on tugging on his leash.

Regina had just sent a pebble skimming across the glassy water where it skipped once, twice, before it hit something in the middle of the river – a bundle of clothes trapped by a tree limb half-submerged, unsettlingly still. Baskerville's growl deepened, and then it turned.

A pale face surrounded by a pale halo of hair and twisted limbs.

***

We made the call, and the police came. All the while, I was unable to tear my eyes from the body and the tree. The gnarled bark of the tree seemed to almost form a grinning face, leering at us as the roots beneath drank the sinking blood. Sirens pierced the heavy quiet, and the lights flashed red and blue against the river and woodlands. The officers barely paused in their ritual – no questions, no need for bystander statements as they prepared their cordons in practiced silence.

The walk home was silent, punctuated only by Baskerville's occasional low growl. Inside, the sounds of laughter, warmth, and incongruity greeted us: Mother and Rosemary sharing a late lunch,

"Old Bridge Park," Mother repeated slowly when we told them. "By an old tree… a holly, perhaps."

"How very odd," she murmured, voice softened but grip steady. "I'll call Tom Keyne."

Tom Keyne arrived with the poise of a man practised in tragic ordinariness. "A mugging gone wrong," he said, punctuating the phrase with a measured regret. "Alex Weston. Eighteen. Such a terrible shame."

Chapter Nine

17th December, 2023
London to Yorkshire
5 days till the murder

By mid-December, the cold had settled in, the cold that burrows itself into your bones and refuses to leave. Snow had fallen steadily, thick drifts blanketing the grey skies and turning the streets into a slushy mire, clinging stubbornly to boots and coats.

I had never been a winter person; I was perpetually mourning the sunlit days, the vibrant greens, the languorous stretch of golden evenings. Winter arrived like a thief, stealing light and warmth, and leaving in its place a landscape stripped bare, dressed in unforgiving grey.

We spent those days mostly indoors, at each other's houses, with Regina and Fiona buzzing with plans for the ball – dresses, shoes, blah blah. The shadows of Alex Weston and Moira Barking faded into distant, almost forgotten echoes, ghosts of a summer that had already grown faint. I, for my part, buried myself in football, friends, and endless matches of FIFA on Archie's PS12.

Christmas break began on the seventeenth. I awoke that morning from a dream of dread, unshaped and slippery: a stranger arriving in the dead of winter.

Later, we drove into Yorkshire under rain not yet surrendered to snow. Cresting the final hill, Rook Manor sprawled beneath us like a vast, ancient creature. Close up, orderly but from a distance, a labyrinthine marvel of stone and history, as though it had risen organically from the moor itself.

My ancestral seat, nearly a thousand years old, had evolved through fire and siege. Baroque and Gothic and something older, wrapped around a central tower that rises almost a twin to

The Rook Woods, lush and alive come summer, now sleep in winter's grip. Life's sounds muted, birds fled elsewhere, leaving only the persistent, strangely louder whistling wind. As the car rumbled along, Old Jack's Hill, a jagged sentinel, watched as we rolled by.

And then, a figure moved atop the tor: a vague, greyish shape against an even greyer sky. Head, shoulders, limbs poised either to watch the car or stare into Fox Hollow. A silent ghost or merely a wanderer seeking solace, most likely, but *this* year's strange events, the sudden death, the aunt, the cryptic flowers Regina found, all seemed to come rushing back.

That night, Granny and I dined in the drawing room with news of record snowfalls and solar storms bending the atmosphere out of joint. Granny was oddly upset about the whole party and seemed dead set against it.

"I do not understand why your mother insists on this party," she said, voice tinged with something like worry.

"It's only a Christmas party," I replied. "Mother's eager for her Academy reunion. What harm could there be?"

"Not the weather, but the people," she said. "So many gathered with wine and no consequences. Storms like this turn men into beasts."

I laughed, too young to fully grasp the weight of her words. "They're well born, surely you don't fear them."

She sighed. "You don't know them as I do. And these storms… they never bode well."

I changed the subject reluctantly. "Granny, how did Aunt Dahlia die?"

Her composure faltered. "Why would you ask such a thing, sweet boy?"

"I just wondered. Forgive me."

She stared for a moment, then told of a fall from a horse. "I warned her not to go out that day. She never listened."

The room fell to silence, broken only by the hearth's low crackle and the moor's mournful breath outside. Finally, she said, "Time for bed, sweetheart."

Chapter Ten

19th December, 2023
2 days to the murder

The rain was that nagging, half-sleet kind, the sort that coats the air in damp chill and makes the stones slick beneath one's feet, the day the Barkings arrived at Rook Manor. Mother and I stood on the slick driveway, umbrellas braced against the wind, as a sleek black car circled the fountain before coming to a halt. Lord Barking was out almost before the engine had stopped, his long coat billowing. He tossed his keys to Flavio, then wrapped Mother in a hug. Their hands lingered clasped, and reluctantly, when they finally parted.

Turning to me, Lord Barking's grin was warm and almost paternal as he clapped me on the shoulder. "Hamlet," he said, and pulled me into a rough hug.

Behind them, Electra and Nicholas emerged from the car, both hunched and sharp-eyed. It had been nearly five months since I'd seen them. Nicholas, usually marked by a lazy cockiness, now wore a hard, cold gaze. I offered my hand, but he ignored it, brushing past me with a deliberate bump. "Mind your step, Barking," I said, holding his gaze until he looked away and stalked indoors. Electra, the politer of the siblings, stepped forward and took my hand briskly. "Good to see you, Rook," she said.

A woman followed them, Sarah Smith, or 'Carly', as she insisted.

Mother had three smiles: her genuine smile, reserved for family and those she loved; her polite smile, used for day-to-day diplomacy; and her third, cold and razor-edged, which she saved for business rivals (or in rarer instances for me when I'm caught in a lie). It was a cutting smile that let you know she knew you couldn't hide from her.

"You've met the son and heir, Hamlet," Lord Barking said, nodding toward me. Carly's hug was unexpected but brief.

My attention was drawn to Nicholas, who was watching with hawk-like intensity. His expression was feral, calculating, as though dissecting their every move.

Lunch unfolded under a veil of brittle civility. Even Mother and Lord Barking, who tend to be rather gregarious in each other's company, were rather quiet. The pair of them seemed soaked in a nervous sort of trepidation. Lord Barking's leg bounced, making a rather maddening tapping sound that echoed off the floorboards, and Mother's fingers toyed and twisted with the stem of her wine glass.

When Carly asked about the manor's dungeons, perhaps innocent curiosity… perhaps trying to break the silence, Mother's smile did not reach her eyes.

"Oh yes," she said lightly, "we use them now for wine." The irony was sharp beneath the surface. Carly's shock was genuine but brief.

"They were reserved for murderers, traitors, and spies," Mother said softly, her voice dropping to a slow hiss. "Their term served until the executioner called."

Lord Barking chimed in, approving the harshness of past punishments and lamenting modern leniency in muted tones. Carly's appetite waned; her eyes flicked to Nicholas, who avoided her gaze.

A long silence followed, broken by Mother's forced chuckle and a pivot to lighter topics: the upcoming party, and whatnot. Nicholas remained distant, and Carly's glass refilled steadily.

Finally, relief arrived, a chance to escape. Mother asked me to show the guests to their rooms, then excused herself to badger the caterers. I was eager to flee the stifling atmosphere.

Lord Barking claimed a large room beside Mother's, steeped in history; Henry VIII himself had reputedly occupied it. Carly was a last-minute company, afforded a smaller room with a view over the northern gardens. Nicholas and Electra clustered near their father.

Electra, ever disarmingly direct, demanded a tour of my room.

She took in the clutter, settled onto the couch, and broached the subject of Carly with a mixture of amusement and disdain. Carly, she said, was more than a tutor: chauffeur, household manager, photographer's muse and, it seemed, aspiring Duchess of London.

"Nicholas adores her," Electra mused, whispering constantly in her corner. "Poor thing."

Nicholas returned her gaze with pure loathing, a mirrored distaste that only siblings can know.

"So, how many guests?" Electra asked.

"Around seventy," I said. "A mix of parents and peers. The plan is a large sleepover, though you're entitled to your own room, unless you'd like to join us."

"I'd love to," Electra sighed.

But Nicholas cut in sharply, "I'll pass."

"You're a handful," Electra teased, rolling her eyes. "Mother's death hit him hard, though he's been… difficult since birth." And with that, she excused herself.

In that sprawling house, beneath weathered stone and history's weight, the quiet power plays of a family endured. And I was trapped, participant and observer alike, in the tangled dance of loyalty and disdain.

That night, sleep came easily, and my dreams carried me back to London's fog-cloaked streets. I wandered past empty towers and shuttered homes until I found myself at the gates of the Rolling Rock, stepping into the church graveyard with legs that felt foreign, unfamiliar. A hand on my shoulder spun me around: Lady Moira Barking, pale in life and paler in death, her slender finger raised, pressing deep into my shoulder. Shapes materialized from the mist, figures in flowing white robes, twirling in silent dance. No dread, no fear, only a strange déjà vu, a vision half-remembered from the dreams within dreams.

Then a sudden crash shattered the illusion. I woke to find Nicholas halfway up the stairs, his face twisted with fury, hot words trailing after Miss Smith as she climbed ahead. His voice, low and snarling: "How dare you? This is not what we agreed… I already paid—"

He seized her arm, spinning her with fierce intensity, until Electra's sharp voice halted him: "Nicholas, that is no way to treat someone!" she cried, peeking out from her door. He spun around and saw her. And then saw me, his expression wild and half-formed, caught between rage and realisation. And, he broke away, storming upstairs, leaving the air thick with unsettled anger.

Miss Smith, shaken yet composed, laughed nervously, dismissing the incident as Nicholas's unfortunate temperament. Electra pressed her gently for more, only to be met with disclosure: she would be leaving the household soon, her duties complete. As she retreated, a sudden crash below halted us, the shattering of a marble bust. On the balcony above, a shadow lingered briefly before vanishing into darkness.

Sarah Smith's face blanched, her gaze fixed on the ruin. Moments later, Mother and Lord Barking burst in, the room charged with questions and muted accusations.

Miss Smith's desperate, "He tried to kill me!" was only met with cold dismissal from Lord Barking and forced, cautious rationalisation from Mother. I wanted to speak of the shadow, the impossible physics of the statue's fall, Nicholas's presence on the stairs, but silence prevailed, the unspoken truths curling in the corners like smoke.

Chapter Eleven

21st December, 2023
Day of the murder

The morning unfurled in a steady stream of arrivals, each guest marked by the chime of introductions and the occasional hug or pat on my shoulder. I spent the day afoot, flitting between groups alongside Mother. Sir Hugh Drinkwater arrived early and received a rather enthusiastic hug from my mother. I shook his hand, a man who had known me since I was at knee-height and regaled us with a scandalous incident involving Baskerville, a drunken puppy at my grandfather's sixtieth birthday at Number 10.

The De Winters were fashionably late. Regina slipped past Mother with familiar purpose, wrapping me in an affectionate, almost inescapable hug. Colin soon joined, with his trademark bone-crushing; Lady De Winter sighed, half-amusement, half-exasperation, "Three days apart, and as if it's been thirty years!"

"The others are in the old dining room," I informed, leading the trio. But Regina insisted on a detour to my room first, taking a bulky garment bag from Rowan De Winter, Regina's brother, more her mirror than Colin's. Rowan, the solitary one, preferred his iPad to the crowd, delivering a typical awkward fist bump before retreating into quietude.

Colin collapsed onto my bed, catching a wrapped box I tossed his way, gifts for our upcoming life as Academy roommates: the obligatory 'World's Best Roommate' mugs, exchanged like secret handshakes. Regina gifted me a delicate glass terrarium box.

"Hamlet, be a dear help?" Her pink gown emerged, and I helped her put it on. Colin excused himself, not willing to muddle affairs of fashion.

Once alone, Regina's voice dipped conspiratorially: "Lord Barking's traitor is surely here. Their greed for exposure will betray them."

I played the sceptic. "If there even is a traitor. For all we know, it is nothing more than the paranoid wanderings of a mind in grief."

"Oh, darling," she rolled her eyes. "Boring. And as for the imposter," her eyes sparkled in the mirror's reflection, "there's only one outsider tonight."

"Sarah Smith?"

"Precisely. Lord Barking's reason for bringing her here is no kindness."

I mentioned Miss Smith's desire to leave early, curtailed by the storm and Lord Barking's insistence. Regina sighed theatrically. "Then we must charm her before she's gone."

She swept from the room like a heroine scripted for intrigue, and I followed into the growing hum of the first-floor hallway, commandeered as a makeshift salon. Pool and ping-pong tables flanked scattered ottomans, a scene Mother would have vetoed, had pressing matters not consumed her.

Laughter flickered, overlaying the undercurrent of tension that threaded through the gathering. Regina spun theories, her charm undimmed. Fiona, noting our exchanged gifts with a hint of envy, prompted a repartee about the fate of Regina's original shoes in the puddle of Alex Smith's blood, and the prudence of keeping spares. Duffy St Brelade interjected, darkly amused by the notion of meeting one's untimely end in anything but one's own drawing room.

Our conversation, which was admittedly a bit irreverent, was cut short when Nicholas Barking's glass struck the floor. His voice, low and unfiltered, carved through the room: "Since Mother died, I see all of you for what you truly are, and I will make you pay!"

Several voices rose in protest, admonishing his bitterness and demanding an apology. Yet Nicholas doubled down, condemning us all as "rotten creatures utterly incapable of introspection," his gaze sharp and unsettlingly fixed on me.

Colin's sardonic laugh broke the tension, "Introspection? What is that? Some kind of foreign dish?" I stepped forward, ready to quell the storm or punch his lights out, but Percival Beauregard-Finch's steady hand on my shoulder held me back.

Nicholas, flushed but resolute, accused us of discrediting dissenters through every means. Percival's retort, a low growl about spin doctors, elicited smirks. Regina stood, eyes twinkling but voice soothing. "Remember, darlings, Nicholas is scarcely himself; grief has unmoored him. His venom is misdirected, not meant truly for us."

As the moment stretched, Mother's arrival shattered the charged silence. "Come, children. Dinner is served."

Chapter Twelve

21st December, 2023
8 p.m.
Night of the murder (Fiona refers to it as the 'unalivement' which I shall not)

Dinner was served in the ballroom, where four long tables had been set in a precise square. The delicate china and silverware caught the flickering glow of the hearth and the scattered Christmas candles, casting a warm orange light that danced across the table. Mistletoe and holly festooned the chandeliers and wreathed the walls, while snow and wind outside tapped against the windowpanes like ghostly fingers.

Around the table, the dress was unexpectedly casual, men in polo shirts and slacks, women in simple skirts and dresses, all except Regina, who never missed a chance to elevate her ensemble. Electra wore her customary riding habit, of course.

This gathering, among the most powerful people on earth, representing every continent, was a curious scene. CEOs of Fortune 500 companies, diplomats, government officials, and even the Prince and Princess of Wales, all seated under one roof. The word 'traitor', which Lord Barking had bandied about earlier, felt almost absurd in this setting. Yet what united them was more than wealth or power; all had once walked the halls of the same academy, studied beneath the same seasoned teachers, played on the same teams. They shared a past that webbed them together, a shared history with Mother before she was a CEO or a matriarch, when she was just one of their own, a girl among peers carrying secrets no outsider could fathom.

Once seated, Lord Barking ascended. The murmur dimmed, and the chime of his spoon against a champagne glass sliced through the quiet. Tall and composed, he surveyed the room with an inscrutable gaze. Eyes met Mother's for a breath, a silent exchange in possession of some private gravity.

"My friends," he began, voice steady and charged, "we gather here in the home of our beloved Isohel." His smile swept the room. "Friends, indeed, but more than friends, we are family. Over time, many of us have become family in the truest sense."

He paused, letting the meaning hang. "As a family, we share joys and sorrows. We are loyal, protective, and we keep each other's secrets, as a family must."

The room's silence deepened, the walls seeming to listen. "And surely," he continued, "members of a family do not betray one another. A house divided cannot stand. If there is someone among us undermining that house, well, we must deal with them."

Cheers erupted, glasses clinked with enthusiastic assent. The tide of noise threatened to overwhelm. But Nicholas remained a still point beside his father, fingers nervously playing with a wine glass stem, his expression enigmatic and taut, dissonant amid the celebration. Miss Sarah Smith sat near him, pale and withdrawn.

Leaning close, Regina whispered, brow arching, "Paranoid wanderings, indeed."

Before I could respond, the sharp crash of breaking glass reverberated. All eyes turned to Nicholas, who had launched from his chair, his father's wine cascading across the carpet like spilled blood. He stood, trembling with fury, voice low and venomous.

"I know the truth," he declared, words slicing the clamour. "I know what you've done. What both of you have done!" His gaze flicked from his father to my mother.

A hush descended, whispers stilled under the weight of accusation.

"I know the truth," he repeated, louder now, voice cracking with resolve. "And I will prove it!" Pointing first at Lord Barking, then at Mother, he declared, "Both of you. All of you!" His voice echoed, sharp and wild, filling the cryptic silence.

Miss Sarah Smith choked, while Nicholas's face drained to the pale of fresh snow. His eyes flickered from the shattered glass to the wine held in her trembling hand. Without another word, he bolted for the door.

Electra seized his wrist. He turned to face his father, then, momentarily losing its edge, like a child dreading chastisement before fixing a defiant glare on his father. Lord Barking's gaze was a sovereign's calm, and I flinched. A nod to Electra, and Nicholas was gone. And Miss Smith continued to choke till Sir Hugh thumped her on the back.

Lord Barking half-smiled. "Well then, shall we continue?"

The conversation resumed, and the storm momentarily passed.

Regina's glance toward me was laden with unspoken commentary, cut short by a sudden intrusion: "Oh, hello, Hamlet," Mr St James, seated beside me, sparked a new interaction. Tall, blonde, with a scruffy beard that lent a rakish charm, alongside his delicate, warm-eyed wife, they were the founders of Second Eden.

"Your mother spoke much of you and your remarkable memory," he said, appraising me as if I were an intriguing specimen.

Regina smiled. "Hamlet went through a phase wanting to be an astronaut."

Mr St James's lips curved into an amused smile. "Second Eden is more than space exploration. It's about saving humanity."

"A poetic and noble sentiment," Regina replied.

He extended an invitation to their office, mentioning a brain scan, eyes not quite meeting mine, "I shall find the time," I murmured.

"Launch is February," he said.

Regina smiled, "That's all terribly fascinating, isn't it, Hamlet?"

"Yes," I responded, uncertain.

Mr St James asked if I still wished to be an astronaut.

"Oh god, no," I said, perhaps too emphatically. "I'm far too fond of earth. I'll miss the trees, the woods, and I'm not for long journeys; I get fidgety on the drive from London."

They laughed, though I knew my words were not truly funny.

Fortunately, Archie Aston, across from Mr St James, began a new conversation.

Regina whispered, "Oh, look at the mouse squirming." We turned to Miss Sarah Smith: pale-faced, eyes darting, playing nervously with her food.

Suddenly, a loud pop and startled wail broke the mood. Lord Bellingham-Frost had uncorked champagne too close to the jumpy Miss Smith.

She rose angrily above the laughter. "Excuse me, I'd like to retire now."

"Poor thing," Mother murmured. "Hamlet, will you see her to her room? Make sure she doesn't lose her way."

I escorted her. She entered and bolted the door without a word. Terribly rude, but perhaps understandable.

Chapter Thirteen

21st December, 2023
An hour till the murder
The Greenhouse

After dinner, Mother, Lord Harry, and a few of their friends settled into a game of poker, the table scattered with half-empty wine glasses and little dishes of marchpane and sugared plums. My friends and I, however, were preparing for an evening decidedly livelier than card play. Mother's voice called across the room, "Do try to include Nicholas. He's been away from the others for a while, and the poor fellow seems rather upset."

"Of course, Mum," I said, biting back the memory of my own very public outburst, an incident that would surely have earned me a week's grounding had it been me sulking in front of the assembled guests.

Lord Barking, looking up from his cards, added with mild irritation, "Where is Nicholas? Returned from his temper tantrum yet?"

"He's probably in his room," I said. "Shall I check?"

"Do, just don't force him to join you. He prefers his solitude when he's sulking."

Before I could reply, Regina stood abruptly, tapping her crystal glass with a dessert fork. The sharp, clear note silenced our murmuring group. "Now, my friends," she declared, eyes sparkling, "It's time for the second act."

Cheers followed, and one by one, our friends rose, drifting off to change. Granny, in one of her more eccentric whims, had installed a natural pool in the greenhouse that autumn, a grand project involving landscape artists and specialists in crafting 'wild spring-fed ecosystems'. Regina, of course, had promptly claimed it as the perfect venue for a pool party.

Hallways filled with the shuffle of luggage and the murmur of half-closed doors as everyone hunted for swimwear. I lingered a moment in the cooler hush beyond the ballroom before ascending to the west wing.

There, Regina and Rowan were locked in a quiet argument, he fiddling with his headphones, eyes darting to the crowd beyond. "It's all so loud," he whimpered.

Regina opened her mouth to protest, but I gently tugged her hair. "Let him be, Reggie. Rowan, you can go wherever you like."

He smiled and slipped away, while the rest headed to the greenhouse. I, however, needed to seek out Nicholas, hidden away in self-imposed exile.

At his door, I knocked softly. "Barking? Are you there?" No answer. Regina tried as well, batting eyelashes coyly. "Nicholas, darling…?"

When the door swung open to reveal an empty, silent room, Regina shrugged. "He'll appear eventually, somewhere dark and far away. Now, let's not keep our friends waiting." Her arm slid through mine.

The party in the greenhouse pulsed with energy: laughter, bursts of shouting, volleyballs in flight. Speakers pumped music against the glass walls, a throng dancing in pale, flickering light.

Moonless and clouded, the thick glass spurned what little light there was. Nearby, the house's distant glow offered only thin, yellow shadows flickering on familiar faces.

Regina and Fiona joined the throng, shaking, spinning, voices ringing, entranced by something primal, the music's pulse syncing with their own bloodbeats. In that moment, surrounded by the scent of earth and wood, I half-believed we were part of an ancient rite, the *Björk* playing like an old fire drum.

I weaved through the crowd and stumbled into Karan Singh and Riya Malhotra's selfie swirl.

"Steady on?" Karan said, smirking as his arm caught my shoulder.

"Sorry, I can barely see in here. Regina and I should've strung fairy lights." I thought then of Karan's recent misfortune. "I'm sorry about your father."

He grinned, the lilt of amusement softening his voice. "The flowers your mother sent did so brighten the hospital room."

"Any progress?" I ventured, fumbling for words to offer comfort.

"Not worsening. Mostly just breathing, beeping. Friends visit when they can."

I nodded, awkward. "It's been a hard year, hasn't it?"

Regina, stepping from the shadows, added quietly, "Tragedy seems to come in threes. What next?"

Riya's dark eyes gleamed. "Speaking of Lady Barking, Karan and I were among the last to see her alive."

Before Regina spoke, a scream ruptured the air. Colin recoiled into glass, the room pausing mid-breath. Polly stood, still and pale, staring into the fogged window.

"You good, Polls?" a nervous voice offered.

She shook her head, breathless. "Someone's there… I saw them walking."

Heads turned, Colin pressed his face to the glass. "No one. The grounds are empty."

"I swear," Polly insisted, "they were just there, by the greenhouse."

"Oh, Polly," Regina sighed, composure regained. "Steam and shadows. Don't be dramatic."

Yet, her eyes lingered long on the window.

Chapter Fourteen

21st December, 2023
The Greenhouse
The murder

That night, without warning, the warm glow of the house flickered twice before vanishing altogether. The carefully strung fairy lights along the hedges, over stone balustrades and iron fences, died instantly, plunging the manor, its grounds, and the greenhouse into near-complete darkness.

A breathless silence settled, as if the shadows had pressed a hand over every mouth. Then came an uncertain voice: "Is the power out?" Regina's sharp, dry retort cut through the gloom. "No, Duffy. Hamlet and I planned to plunge you all into darkness as a festive prank. Merry Christmas."

Nervous laughter flickered. Phones glowed with flashlights, casting feeble blue halos in the dark. Outside, snow tapped softly on the glass ceiling, but the greenhouse air felt stifling, as if the building itself held its breath.

James, standing beside me, offered a practical theory. "The storm must have knocked out a transformer."

Colin snorted. "A transformer? Like Megatron?"

I walked to the glass walls and saw the path's lamp posts still lit, their halos haloed by the fogged glass. "The power's not out," I said. "Only the house has lost electricity. Someone must have switched it off."

"Too many murder mysteries," Archie said, ever the sceptic. "Likely just a tripped breaker. Your mother's servants will fix it. Though I wouldn't mind if they took their time, it does add a certain romance."

Suddenly, Polly screamed. A blurred silhouette darted past the fairy lights, stumbling against the glass with a heavy thud, muffled gasps following.

The figure pressed against the pane for a second, a distorted, faceless blur, then righted itself and raced into the night, leaving behind only a faint smudge and an uneasy silence.

"See?" Polly shrieked.

I forced a shrug, goosebumps prickling my skin. "Probably a servant coming to restore the power."

We waited, breath held. Duffy shuddered. "The storm's really picking up."

"Storm of the century," Colin echoed.

The darkness deepened; branches scraped and rattled against the windows.

"Shouldn't someone be fixing the electricity?" Fiona whispered.

It struck me then: "The servants left after dinner. They're off celebrating Christmas. I'll go."

Slipping out, Baskerville at my heel, I grabbed a torch. Outside, the cold was immediate, brutal, as snow thickened, swallowing paths and hedgerows in a muffled white shroud. The torch's narrow beam cut through drifting flakes, illuminating frost-laced gates and the delicate lacework of winter. Baskerville puffed little clouds from his nose, lead taut in my hand.

I've never feared the dark; there is nothing that isn't present in the light. Yet something about the silencing snow and the distant, blurred manor pressed sharply against my nerves.

At the trellis, a breaker box hidden behind ivy-covered stone, I crouched, brushed snow off, and flipped the switch. Life returned, warm lights flared through windows, and inside, bright holiday music began anew, almost jarringly cheerful.

Relieved, I rounded a corner and froze. A woman lay sprawled in the snow, limbs askew. Snow settled on her lashes. It was Miss Sarah Smith. Pale, motionless, the pure snow unstained by any blood.

I stared long enough to imagine breath, a faint stir. Turning away to fetch help, Baskerville barked sharply. A shadow flashed by, and then a blow struck my head, bursting my vision. Suddenly, I was on the ground, dimly aware of Baskerville's roars and the vanishing shadow.

How long I lay, I cannot say. But his wet nose pushed me upright. Head ringing, vision swimming, I saw her still there, close enough, almost to touch, as if her cold fingers reached out from death's embrace.

I forced my feet beneath me and stumbled back inside through the drawing room window.

A soft voice pulled me fully awake.

"Goodness. Are you quite alright?" Electra was on the phone.

"Ow," was all I managed to say.

She studied me with concern. "Were you outside? I was talking with Barnaby Abernathy-Heath. He just broke up with his girlfriend; I was feeling sorry for him."

My stomach twisted. Electra's worry was a warm cloak.

"I'll find your mother," she promised.

Mother and Lord Barking came rushing in, boots echoing on the cold night floors.

"Get a doctor," I heard someone say, but I shook my head.

"No... no... I'm fine."

Mother pressed a glass into my hand; I swallowed without taste. When I looked up, their pale, worried faces were bent toward me.

"What happened, darling?"

I closed my eyes, breathing deep. "I went to fix the lights... and behind the house, I found Miss Smith lying in the snow and then someone hit me. I fell."

Mother's face was unreadable. "Are you sure it was Sarah Smith?"

Lord Barking sighed, rubbing his neck. "She's locked in her room. I just checked. The door is locked from the inside. Assumed she was asleep."

I said nothing. The image of her face in the snow churned in my stomach.

Regina burst in. "Where were you, Hamlet?"

Mother was silent for a moment, then said quietly, "Perhaps we should check."

Coats were fetched, and into the snow we went again. Cold numbed the ache in my head.

But at the spot where she'd lain, there was nothing. Only snow swirling in the golden pool of light from the house.

Mother and Lord Barking exchanged glances, silent.

"But she was right there," I said, desperation creeping in.

Mother laughed, dry and brittle. "Perhaps you hit your head harder than you realise."

Before I could speak, Lord Barking knelt to brush snow aside. Something metallic caught the light; he held it close.

Her face tightened upon seeing it.

He looked up and nodded at me. Above, a third-floor window stood open, curtains flailing wildly in the wind.

Chapter Fifteen

Regina and I trailed behind, our footsteps softened by the thick carpet, as Mother knocked gently on the closed door. Her voice was low and steady, calling Sarah's name once, twice, several times. Silence greeted us. Mother pressed her ear against the door with quiet intent, listening for any sign of movement. After a long pause, she straightened and pronounced, "Nothing."

Rosemary, with a frown of concern, ventured, "Unusual... does anyone here know how to pick a lock?"

Regina barely hesitated, extracting my monogrammed handkerchief and deftly sliding it under the door. With the poise of one accustomed to small subversions, she borrowed a pen from Lord Barking's pocket, inserted it into the keyhole, and tapped sharply. The click of metal rang through the silence. She withdrew the handkerchief to reveal a small key resting on top. "Voilà!" she announced quietly, victorious.

Lord Barking, Rosemary, and Mother exchanged impressed glances. I gave Regina a respectful pat on the back. With a nod, Lord Barking slid the key home and opened the door.

The room was empty. The window stood wide, allowing winter's icy breath to creep inside.

"Are you sure she locked herself in here, son?" Lord Barking's voice was low, cautious.

I swallowed. "Yes. I brought her up after dinner; she locked the door. Then we left for the greenhouse."

Mother drifted to the window, studying the darkness outside before snapping it shut decisively. "How long was it between when you brought her here and when you noticed she was gone?"

"Not long," I said, exchanging a glance with Regina. "We'd just returned. The sprinklers started... Polly screamed."

"Polly Shrewburry? Why did she scream?" Mother's voice sharpened.

"She said she saw someone on the grounds."

"And then the lights went out," Regina added. "Polly screamed again. This time, we all saw it, a shadow passing the greenhouse, heading toward the front of the house. It was quick, twenty minutes, maybe."

Mother absorbed the details silently, brows furrowed. A floorboard creaked behind us. We turned to see Sir Hugh standing in the doorway, a knowing look shared with Mother. He smiled faintly. "Perhaps the children should return to their party."

Mother nodded, an unspoken relief passing between us, and we found our way back.

"It is quite the coincidence," Fiona said, half dry, half serious, "that you find yet another dead body and forget to call us."

I frowned. "What good would that do? My first thought upon finding a corpse wouldn't be 'I should phone Fiona.'"

Polly pouted. "We could be helpful."

"Oh? How so?"

"Emotional support," she offered.

"You're not being supportive now."

Before she could respond, a shape bumped me in the dark. "Goodness, Nicholas!" Polly breathed. "Where've you been?"

In the dim glow, Nicholas appeared, shaken, breath urgent.

"We haven't seen you since before dinner," Archie said. "You threw your tantrum and stormed off. Finished your sulk, have you?"

Nicholas offered no answer. His gasps and tremors seemed almost like tears. Regina stepped close, clasping his hands. "Leave him be, the poor dear is shivering." Together, they walked away.

Twenty minutes later, the water-fueled chaos had subsided. The others changed and bathed, and we gathered in the emptied ballroom, sleeping bags drawn close.

The mood shifted toward tales of 'maybe dead', 'maybe vanished' women, and ghost stories, shaped by the storm and the week's gloomy palette.

Archie, grinning his signature Aston grin, challenged us to tell each other a ghost story. "A grand old time," he promised. "The ancient Victorians made it a Christmas tradition."

Yuki, cradled in Polly's arms, chuckled. "The ancient Victorians, did they? Do tell, Archie."

"Hush," Archie admonished, eyes twinkling. "We're in a manor older than most countries, in the storm's heart. I am determined to make Duffy cry."

Colin recounted Irish tales of a banshee – the lament heard on stormy nights, glimpsed just out of the corner of the eye.

Regina told the tale of The Sleeping Court: lords and ladies ensnared in eternal slumber beneath blooming hawthorns, their beauty preserved untouched by time, a story more fairytale than ghost story.

I rested my head in Regina's lap, feeling her fingers stroke my hair. "Hammy, tell them about the stranger in the night, the devil in the manor… your grandfather's tale."

I sat up, excitement blooming. "Old Scratch himself, an ancient name for the devil, visited Lord Rook right here on the solstice."

"The servants entered with a tall, hooded stranger pleading sanctuary from the cold," I said. "Lord Rook, cold and godless, ordered him cast out. The stranger offered a bargain, a card game. If Rook won, he'd leave; if he lost, the stranger would stay. My ancestor was clever. He saw beneath the cloak, cloven hooves, and recognised the stranger was no man but Satan himself."

A log popped; Colin screamed. Laughter followed.

"The stranger promised to bless the House of Rook with fame, wealth, and power if he lost. Well, obviously Lord Rook won," I said, allowing myself a smirk, "Look at me."

Some laughter sounded, and I went on, "Through cunning, Rook prevailed, enraging the devil who tore off his cloak and vowed to return once each generation to claim a Rook child, leaving that scorch mark which endures."

I gazed from the ballroom windows toward the snow-cloaked moor. "The devil fled, scattering cards which fell to form Old Jack's Tor."

There was a chatter of voices, and those who had seen the tor on mother's summer vegan hunting parties disagreed: some said it resembled a handful of playing cards, and others said it was just a pile of rocks.

Colin, apparently quite eager to prove his bravado, laughed, “What a load of rubbish.”

“Says the person who screamed like a little girl a moment ago.”

“Oh shut it, Hamlet!”

Archie’s logic tempered the tale, “The tor is just ancient rocks, and the ceiling burn could be any mundane household maladies.”

“Perhaps,” I admitted, “but the mark returns, shape and place unchanging, despite centuries of repairs. I remember when the ceiling collapsed when I was seven. The fresh plaster still bore the mark.”

Oh come, Hamlet,” Sidd said, “You don’t believe that old wife’s tale?”

All eyes rested on me. I smiled thinly. “Of course not. Just that, a tale.” However, I wasn’t so certain. Grandfather’s rainy-night story haunted my sleep for months; fear of a devil beneath the bed spawned screams and nightly comfort from Mother.

Marianne Montague took the torch, sharing tales of the Old Folk, ‘faeries’ or ‘fae,’ as most call them.

Duffy interrupted, “Like Tinkerbell?”

She spoke of spirits in shadows, reflections, moonlight on snow, sunlight through leaves, tricksters leading men into bogs or over cliffs.

A sudden bright light flashed outside. “Faery lights,” someone whispered.

Archie chuckled. “No, just the car lot. Someone’s going to their car.”

Nicholas, for once, spoke: “I have a story.”

Several nodded. It was his longest address of the evening.

“I assume you know the Graveman?” His voice gathered attention. We nodded, we all knew, after all. A boogeyman of playground legend.

“One two stay in view, three four lock the door, five six candlesticks, seven eight it’s too late, nine ten Graveman’s coming for you then.”

And with that, the night and tales stretched long into the dark.

Chapter Sixteen

That night, the manor crept into my dreams, a summer night, singular, and I was alone. And, like all dreamers, I was possessed of a preordained purpose beyond my own awareness. Ahead, a figure in pale white floated just out of reach. We wound through corridors, descending the grand staircase. I called for her to wait, but she drifted onward, her footsteps ghostly silent against polished floors. She turned briefly, a visage familiar, yet not quite. It was almost Mother, decades younger, sharpened by time and memory, her eyes black ink spilled across vellum.

She smiled over her shoulder and stepped onto the moor, the heather whispering around her skirt. I chased her, but as shadows lengthened, a host of dark, feathered creatures erupted, talons and shrieks swirling around me. They circled close enough to brush my face, their feathers soft as a lover's kiss, yet caused me no harm.

Winter sunlight filtered through my bedroom windows as I awoke, the dream clinging to my mind with eerie tenacity. So vivid was that black-eyed girl, so like my mother, that I half-expected her to linger in the corner of my room. I told myself then that it had just been the strange events of the previous night with Miss Sarah Smith and the ghost stories and whatnot. But I felt, even then, a sense of anticipation that bordered on dread, and I ignored it.

Around me, the household stirred. Gentle footsteps and the wash of awakening filled the manor. We gathered in the great hall for breakfast, where the scent of pinecones crackling in the hearth mingled with tea warmed by tiny flickering lights; platters of eggs, sausages, and toast lay beneath the high windows.

Regina and Fiona conferred with the girls' accustomed enthusiasm over dresses and makeup, while Colin, never a morning person, was listlessly spooning bits of egg into his mouth.

Mother rose, clearing her throat with quiet authority. The murmur of awakening conversation stilled. "I am sure you have all heard of the mysterious events last night," she began. "A guest under my roof, Sarah Smith, has disappeared into the storm. We have informed the Great Sacrifice Police Department, which is investigating a woman who went missing in the tempest. I cannot say what transpired, but I am certain it was nothing... untoward."

A ripple of murmurs followed.

"While we keep Miss Smith in our prayers, we must not allow this tragedy to overshadow our celebration. The weekend will proceed as planned."

Regina's eyes met mine briefly before I turned back to my food. After breakfast, as I trailed my friends toward the game room, Mother's fingers closed gently on my shoulder. "Sweetheart, a word."

In her office, seated behind her desk, she awaited me. Lord Barking appeared, dragging Nicholas by the shoulder. "Sit," he said sharply. Nicholas obeyed, his face a flash of hatred and indignation – a sight that brightened my spirits momentarily.

"Hamlet," Mother began conversationally, "exactly when did you see Miss Smith in the snow?"

I looked at them – Mother, Lord Barking, Nicholas – and found no easy answer. "I don't know. I had no watch or phone."

"Think," Mother pressed. "What time?"

"After dinner, some two hours, perhaps more. I don't know."

Lord Barking shrugged. "Dinner began at 7:45 and concluded by 8:45. Nicholas had his tantrum. You accompanied that woman to her room around 8:20. You're certain she locked the door?"

"Yes," I replied, "I heard the lock click."

Lord Barking's voice was steady, probing. "What happened after that? Tell us precisely."

"I returned to dinner, and we set off immediately to the greenhouse. Polly saw the figure. The lights went out; we all saw it. I went to restore the lights. On returning, I found her in the snow, headed for help when someone struck me from behind… t'was a busy night."

Mother and Lord Barking shared a long, silent look – an almost telepathic exchange.

"One last question, Hamlet," Lord Barking said. "Your mother and I asked you to find Nicholas. Did you?"

"Regina and I did. We knocked, but no one answered."

Mother's voice softened. "Nicholas? Where were you, dear?" Nicholas and his father stared. A tense standoff before the boy dropped his gaze.

"Yes. Where were you?" Lord Barking's tone was quietly angry. "Not in your room. Not with the others. Where?"

"In the library," Nicholas whispered.

"Alone?"

"Yes. Too many people. I needed space."

"Did you leave?"

"No."

A knock at the door announced Regina's voice. "May I come in?" Mother exchanged a glance with Lord Barking and admitted her.

Regina entered, transformed from pyjamas into tweed and crisp white, apologizing with practised charm. "I was with Nicholas last night. Discussing the book he was reading, shortly after Hamlet left to fix the lights. I checked on Nicky to calm his fears."

I stared, jaw slack. We had scarcely parted when I left to restore the power. When she came for me, she wore a swimsuit and a robe. Unless she dressed, conversed, then redonned the swimsuit in fifteen minutes, she was lying. I do not have any great moral compulsion against lying, say in politics and fashion, but not to protect Nicholas Barking!

He studied Regina silently. "Very curious. Nicholas said he was alone in the library the whole time. If you were truly together, why did he omit this?"

Regina paled, chin raised, silence blooming before she spoke again, "He was protecting my honour. Nicholas and I have become… involved. We shared a kiss."

Surprise rippled, Mother, Lord Barking, Nicholas, me, and even Regina.

Nicholas nodded. "She speaks true."

Lord Barking smiled, a mixture of amusement and pride. "Admirable. Every man needs a sharp woman. But how long?"

Their exchanged glance answered.

"Since October," Nicholas admitted. "She reached out by text, and slowly, I fell."

Regina nodded emphatically.

I knew, of course, that this was a bald-faced lie. If Regina had been texting anyone, I would know every single gristly detail, regardless of whether I wanted to or not. I had been staring almost open-mouthed until the toe of her heel met my shin. "Yes," I said so suddenly that Mother and Lord Barking flinched, "Yes. Regina told me about this back in October."

Lord Barking shrugged with a smile. "Just one more thing before you go." He produced a small golden cufflink etched with the Barking crest. "This is yours, Nicholas."

Nicholas swept the token up and left, Lord Barking's gaze trailing his son's retreat.

Once clear of the office, I seized Regina's wrist. "To my room, need your help."

"Of course."

She addressed Nicholas, "Now, my love, join the others in billiards. We'll be down shortly."

In my room, Regina collapsed on my bed. "Oh, Hamlet," she sighed. "Why did I say that?"

"Why indeed? Why lie for Nicholas?"

She smiled defiantly in the mirror. "Don't tell anyone, but he killed that woman."

I staggered. "How do you know that?"

"Who else could it be? He was unaccounted for then. He confessed."

I stammered. "Did he really?"

"Spluttering, yes. Something about white flowers."

"That's thin evidence. If he confessed, why lie?"

Her smile darkened. "Knowledge is power. Keeping Nicholas, the spin doctor's heir, under our thumb is advantageous."

I smirked. "You're describing blackmail."

"A favour exchange, darling. We keep his secret, he does what we want."

Our eyes locked. "You make even blackmail sound… logical."

Chapter Seventeen

22nd December, 2023
Afternoon and evening
Rook Manor

At lunch, we tucked into hearty bowls of beef and barley stew, and I chose to sit with the Darlings, who were abuzz with talk of the academy. Archie, restless and eager, said, "Only twenty days till we move in. I've counted down to this moment for years, but now that we're here, I feel jittery."

I shared his feelings on the matter. The academy was a legacy etched into our family name and home, as entwined as Rook Manor itself. Since its founding in 1587, generations of Rooks had passed through its halls, as had the De Winters, the Barkings, and others whose families had interlaced over the centuries. To attend was to enter a sacred rite, a tradition woven of friendship and power, secrets known within a select circle.

Colin mumbled through a mouthful of mashed potatoes that he'd procured a television for our room, though the rest was lost in the hum of his chewing.

Regina's sigh punctuated the table chatter. "I'm thrilled, naturally, but the uniform! In prep school, at least we had freedom after hours. At the academy, we're shackled to it from dawn till dusk. It's stifling; how can one express oneself?"

I suppressed a grin. One small mercy: no more following Regina's shopping escapades in the city, lugging her ever-growing parcel pile as she eyed shoes and blouses.

Her sip of drink was accompanied by a steady gaze and unspooling worries. "What of the traditions? 'Bartholomew's Voyage,' is it called? I dread the boat, it's awful."

Fidgety Duffy's voice faltered, "Demzela mentioned some kind of initiation, 'student-led', but she wouldn't say what. Should we be worried?"

Colin shot back, "Man up, Duffs. How bad could it be?"

Fiona teased, "Don't be such a baby."

Polly's tone was gentler. "Daily football at 6:30, that's the real concern."

Archie, swearing reformation, promised to rouse Duffy by any means necessary. "Though it might be excessive," Duffy muttered as the room chuckled.

The arrival of Mother commanded attention. She stood, glasses poised, and silence fell as she addressed the room with measured sorrow. "I regret to inform you that Sarah Smith is dead. Authorities have found her near town; she likely perished from exposure. The details remain unclear."

Whispers spread as Regina and I exchanged silent glances, her green eyes sharp.

Mother's voice softened yet filled the room: the wandering child was thought to have escaped through a window, perhaps inebriated or seeking clandestine company, but the cold proved fatal. "Though a stranger, she merits our prayers." The room bowed its head; the pause lingered, poignant and collective.

Later, as the morning gave way to a grey afternoon and mingled conversations resumed, I found solace in the silent woods. Baskerville's steady presence grounded me in the hush of snow-laden trees, the whistle of wind, the muted secrets of the moor.

A flash of metal caught my eye, a phone half-buried in snow. Tapping life into its sluggish screen revealed a picture of the missing woman. The discovery shackled my thoughts; though a dutiful son would have handed it over to mother, but well… I slipped it into my pocket, deciding to show it to Regina later.

Chapter Eighteen

22nd December, 2023
Night after the murder
Rook Manor

The storm had returned with unrelenting fury, and the wind sounded almost human as it came screaming across the moor. So unrelenting that it made the previous night's fall seem like a mere whisper. Now, the world lay swathed in thick, blinding white; from my window, the tree line and the distant moor were swallowed in a pallid fog.

Inside, however, the manor blossomed with festive warmth. Wreaths adorned with ribbons, golden bells, and crystal droplets caught the vibrant twinkles of red, green, and gold lights. The air tasted of pine, cloves, and mulled wine. The crackle of the hearth mingled with laughter, chatter, and fussing over hair and clothes.

Everyone was dressed in full formal regalia for dinner. Mother wore the family tiara of Normandy, a matched suite of diamonds like frozen starlight. Lady De Winter bore the Antrim tiara, its jewels once held by the Romanovs, while the Princess of Wales, formerly Lady Jane Aston-Frost, donned the Cambridge lovers' knot. Across it all, Regina's discourse on these baubles dissolved into white noise against the swirl of my thoughts.

At last, we entered the dining room in order of rank. The Prince and Princess led, followed by Mother and Lord Barking, their station secure as the highest noble family present. Seated last, I absorbed the room's quiet charge.

Mother rose and began, voice clear amid the hush. "Harry called us a family, and if he's right, I want to introduce as the guest of honour this weekend, the man who has been like a father to most of us, Sir Hugh Drinkwater…"

The master of St Bartholomew's Academy stood, taking the room's applause with a modest bow. "He rarely leaves the school grounds, but tonight he obliged, and I thank him."

At one point mother had some Christmas songs played over the stereo. "God rest y'e merry genttlen, let nothing you dismay…"

It was rather loud. Songs and voices and clatter and the roar of storm, I found it hard to focus on anything. People tried to talk to me at a few occasions but nothing really sank through. Perhaps that blow to head rattled me more than I realised.

I said that in the manor we felt quite safe, the outside world almost forgotten… but the outside world did not forget us, and when we were partway through the starters, a maid came in and informed Mother of a guest who had just arrived, claiming to be an old friend. "How very odd," Mother said, perhaps made listless by wine and good conversation, "Although all old friends are welcome. Sweetheart, will you go see who it is?"

"Remember Christ our Savior was born on Christmas Day to save us all from Satan's pow'r when we were gone astray."

I found the stranger in the quiet drawing room, gazing into the fire. His face was marked by time and trouble, one eye glinted blue beneath an eyepatch, and his blonde hair was wild. He smiled, studying me.

"Little Hamlet," he said, voice laden with history. "How you've grown." I stared up at the strange man who had claimed to be an old friend of my mother. I didn't recognise his face, and it was one I wouldn't forget. Yet he spoke with such familiarity.

He was still holding my hand, and his one eye hadn't left my face once. He laughed, "Oh well, that depends on who you ask. I would say yes, but she said no."

There was something odd about the way the stranger was staring at me. As though he was searching for something in my face, something familiar and as though he was in on a joke that I was on the receiving end of.

"Um… so would you like me to take you into the dining hall. The others are at dinner now."

He reclined in his chair and put his legs up on the footrest. "Oh, not yet. Let's chat a little first." I nodded just to be polite, even though I was feeling like I'd much rather be anywhere else than under that gaze of his. But at the same time, I found myself strangely fascinated by the stranger. He was so quiet, unlike everyone else I know, so unlike Mother's other friends with their stiff backs and stiff manners. He sat in that chair with an odd confidence, and I found myself quite unable to look away.

"You must be very excited to start at Old St Barts," he said. "It's a very beautiful place… very beautiful and very old, far out at sea, all alone on that little island. On most days, you can't even see the mainland, and it feels like it's just you, the island, the mist, and the sea. When you're there," he went on, "going around lessons or muddying off to footie practice, you quite forget the rest of the world exists."

His eyes looked out over the moor and the frenzy of rain and wind and scratching tree branches.

"And," he smirked again, "it's both a blessing and a curse, I suppose. We were there during the war. The solitude of the old place kept us quite away from the fighting… but so many of us had brothers and fathers fighting in the war." His voice trailed off again, and he leaned back in his armchair, letting out a long, slow breath.

"How very fascinating... so…" I asked again, "You are one of my mother's friends? She never mentioned you… Mister?"

"Monroe… David Monroe," he said. "You look very much like her, you know?" he said, "The same skin tone, the same eyes."

That is true; I have always been told that I look like a miniature version of her, but the stranger's overfamiliarity and bouncing conversation were beginning to get a bit jarring, so I merely nodded.

He chuckled, "Shall we go to dinner then?"

David stepped in with a broad smile, and as all the adults in the room turned to look at him; he was the only one smiling.

There was a great hush, and the only sounds were the crackling of the fire, the roar of the storm outside and the rattle of the panes.

Mother stood up, her chair scratching discordantly and deafeningly as she did, "David," she said in a dangerous tone, "Why are you here?"

David smiled and approached the table. Pulling out Miss Smith's empty chair, he sat down.

Chapter Nineteen

"Get out!"

The words were Mother's. The man David seemed almost transformed. Gone was the charming, if odd man I'd met; his face had come alive with an almost fanatical hatred. What followed was a terribly undignified display. David made some rather veiled statements. I couldn't catch quite all of it and the music seemed almost jarring now in the silence.

"And there'll be scary ghost stories and tales of the glories of Christmas long, long ago."

He said to Harry, "Poor Sweet Moira… my heart breaks for her…"

For one, he called Sir Hugh "A glorified janitor." And said that he was still "cleaning up after these fools."

He made vague mention of what Second Eden is doing "behind closed doors."

And then he turned to, of all people, my grandmother and said "I notice you two have expunged every trace of her… her garden… her room… everything. But some ghosts are not so easy to exorcise, are they?"

Something went over the room at that. Suddenly no one could look each other in the eye. Hands shook on glasses and silverware.

Some snarled back. Just when it was hitting a fever pitch, Mother had him dragged out. He went with a smile.

There was a long silence. Delicate and taut like a bow string, it stretched, uncomfortable and expectant, until Mother's voice rose, soft but firm, "Perhaps it's best if we discuss this in private. The children should be dismissed."

The room hesitated, a suspended moment of confusion, before the sharp voice of the Princess of Wales shattered the stillness. "You heard her. Out, all of you."

No one argued. The clatter of cutlery ceased, and, as one, we abandoned our seats and filed silently from the room, the plush curtains muffling our footsteps. After all, when a princess commands, even dissent bows.

But not all complied without complaint. Archie, restless, indignant, flung his jacket atop the pool table, pacing with barely constrained fury. "It's preposterous. The adults drone on about preparing us for the real world, yet when serious talk arrives, we're shuttled out like infants. I sat through a marathon meeting about lug nuts – lug nuts! Just last week. But now, when matters truly grip them, we're told we're too young!"

"Oh, Archie," murmured Polly, soothing as ever. "It's not that they doubt us."

"Then what?" Archie shot back.

Regina, perched with elegant disdain, murmured, "Some things are simply too unsavoury for our tender ears. Don't expect business talk; more likely, the subject is that meddlesome David."

"Who, exactly?" asked Windsor, brow furrowed.

"An old friend, apparently," replied Regina. "Not well regarded, judging by their faces."

"Filth," said Fiona, shuddering. "His accusations were base and vile, utterly beneath the company."

Colin's jaw hardened. "I wanted to throttle him for insults to my mother and Lady Rook, but Regina intervened."

"Curious how he knows so much," Duffy whispered uneasily. "Secrets behind closed doors..."

"Secrets, there are none," Archie scoffed. "Only indifference, at best."

“Lies!” shot James. “The space colonies are secure. No one would lose more than my family if anything went wrong.”

“Except the colonists,” Thaddeus interjected, “their families, the investors.”

James bristled, but Felicity St Clair interjected, her voice sharp beneath a steely gaze. “I can attest, my mother and father say otherwise.”

“Religious fanatics,” James spat. “Our labs are scrutinized and sanctioned. The patients were condemned criminals.”

A hush fell, the hearth’s crackle underscoring the weight of revelation.

Regina leaned close, whispering, “Traitors, impostors, spies – a proper litany of woe.”

We retreated into shadowed corridors. “Thrilling, isn’t it? The secrets, the sins, and that David Monroe, quite a feast for the senses.”

“I can’t deny,” I replied, “he is – deliciously dangerous,” Regina cut in with a grin.

A sudden laugh from me sent sparks flying, literally as the wine splashed. Regina shot a warning glance, “Darling, mind your volume.”

She peered toward the closed door. “One wonders what conspiracies unfold behind it.”

“I know,” I whispered, “thanks to a hidden alcove built by a cautious ancestor.”

We slipped through secret passageways, descending into darkness to kneel before a concealed grate overlooking the dining hall.

Voices rose upward: Sir Hugh extolling vigilance over the children; the elders weaving plans and guarding clandestine truths.

“Better the youth remain unaware,” intoned Lady Regal, her tone icy.

The echoes of buried sins whispered through ancient stone walls, stitching shadows and history into a dense tapestry.

And in the flickering firelight, the night deepened as the weight of legacies and betrayals settled once again upon the house of Rook.

Chapter Twenty

January 2024

The tenth of January arrived with surprising suddenness. All this time I'd been counting the days, whittling them off on the diary calendar I got as a stocking stuffer, but as the dawn came stealing through my window, I was rather startled by how quickly the day had come.

All the time I had spent counting down the days, I had forgotten just how much my life was about to change. For the first time, I would be away from Mother, Grandmother, and Old Baskerville. It was Baskerville I was most worried about; he'd never really been without me for longer than I was at school or footie practice. Even on holidays, we'd take him with us.

And on the rare occasion I'd have to go somewhere he couldn't come with me, he'd wait by the door with his big black head on his forepaws, and his big soulful eyes would light up as soon as I walked through the door.

What would he do when I didn't return? Would he understand and find Mother or Grandmother to give him some head pats? Or would he wait endlessly till I returned?

That morning, I buried my face in his fur and tried to explain everything, and I told him that he mustn't wait or be sad, and that I would be back before he knew it.

Eventually, I rose, showered, dressed, and sprayed myself with a lot of deodorant, then went down for breakfast. I had a nervous stomach and only managed a glass of orange juice.

The morning was bright and clear, but I found myself almost wishing for another of those wicked storms just so the whole thing could be delayed.

Mother came down at half past six. Ever since the Christmas party, Mother had been rather jumpy. One night at dinner, a car backfired on the road and in the midst of telling Rosie about whatever funny or unfunny thing had happened at parliament, she leapt out of her seat and spilled her wine on Baskerville.

Mother and I walked to the car, the crunch of gravel beneath our feet swallowed by the winter hush. Once inside, as I strapped myself into the seatbelt, she reached into her pocket and handed me a small green felt box. My heart skipped a beat as I opened it to reveal a signet ring bearing the Rook-Lefey family crest.

She watched wordlessly as I slipped it on immediately, my thumb brushing over the familiar design: a fox and a deer supporting a shield beneath the coronet of a marquis. The shield itself bore an intricate arrangement, an ivy wreath, a key, a cross, a dagger, and, of course, a rook.

I'd been waiting for this moment my entire life. In our family, receiving the ring is a rite of passage, as inevitable as it is significant. Mother had been given hers by my grandfather when she was fourteen, just as he had received his at the same age, and so the tradition continued. As the weight of the ring settled on my finger, I couldn't help but feel its history settle on my shoulders.

I looked up at Mother, not quite sure what to say, but I managed a thanks. She nodded and began the drive, the bodyguards following in their own car.

"I'm relieved it fits," she said, looking at me in the rear-view mirror, "I was worried it wouldn't." She bit her lip before speaking again, "Hamlet, listen to me. Things at the academy are quite different. You can't run around with your uniform unbuttoned and your tie undone as you do at the prep. You certainly can't mouth off to your professors and teachers the way you do to me." (It took great reserves of strength not roll my eyes at this.) She went on as she always does, "And above all, remember that you are a Rook, and on the island, as in the world, you are an ambassador of that legacy. The academy, I, and your peers will expect you to act as such."

I refrained from mentioning that my peers were 'ambassadors' of great legacies themselves, and none of them fit any standards of behaviour and decorum. But I merely nodded, "I know, Mum, I'll try not to let you down."

And yet she still wasn't done, "And, Hamlet, you and your friends will be away from parental supervision for the first time. I know that you all will no doubt experiment in all sorts of things, and I suppose I can't entirely stop you. It's a part of growing up, of course, but do try and keep whatever you do... legal."

We arrived at the pier, driving past the old bridge and high iron fence with the St Barts and St Benedicta crest on the archway, and were waved in by security.

There were scenes of farewell and departure. Duffy, for one, was crying into his mother's arms, and I decided I would not be doing that.

Mother walked me out and helped me unload my trunks. "One more thing, darling," she said, and I turned and looked at her, "Avoid... avoid... avoid any bad influences, okay."

I was a bit confused by the vague statement, but I nodded.

Lord Barking was there too with Nicholas. Nicholas stepped out of the car and walked towards the assembled group with nary a glance back at his father. Lord Barking raised a hand in farewell before dropping it.

Mother and I walked up to him, and he clapped me on the shoulder. "Well, good luck out there, son," he said before leaning into a whisper, "I have no doubt you and the lads have all sorts of mischief planned. But do try not get caught. Spare your mother any phone calls for at least the first week."

I smirked up at him, his presence lighting my mood as it always did. "No promises, Sir."

Sir Hugh was greeting those who came in. He smiled at me, "Ah, there you are...welcome, Lord Hamlet Rook." Mother gave me a quick hug goodbye and her smile altered a fraction, "Sweetheart," she whispered, "Have fun and be careful."

Something in her voice sent a shudder down my back, but I nodded and went to join the others.

I found the Darlings standing together in a tight circle, hoods and jackets drawn up against the salt-scented cold sweeping in from the water.

Then Colin tackled me, and we wrestled till Archie and Duffy pulled us apart.

Regina clicked her tongue, "I expected better of both of you. We are about to leave for the academy, and you still act like children."

Duffy, with his tears now dried, slapped her lightly, "Oh, Reggie, lighten up, we have been watching these two rolling around for about nine years now, I expect to see it continue while we're at the academy, if not, I shall miss it and be terribly sad."

We were in a private sort of waiting area on the water. Behind us was the Old Bridge park looming large and green, and in front of us was the silver-grey expanse of the river. All around us, people were chatting excitedly and milling about, while teams of men moved our luggage for us.

A rather large boat sat waiting for us out on the water.

A handsome old thing built in the style of ships of old, with the St Bart's crest proudly standing out from the sails.

It's called St Bartholomew's Voyage because it follows in the footsteps of St Bartholomew of Oakwood, the saint who, along with his sister St Benedicta, had founded the academy all those centuries ago. The pair apparently made the exact same journey we did when they first set out in the 5th century (I suppose they could call it the voyage St Bartholomew and St Benedicta, but that would be rather a mouthful).

Eventually, Sir Hugh led us in small groups to smaller boats waiting to ferry us to the ship. I got in with the Darlings. Polly almost slipped into the water but managed to grab onto Yuki, and the pair of them fell rather painfully onto the little boat, causing it to rock quite a bit. But other than bruised egos, they were fine.

Once on the main ship, we all sat down to tea and cucumber sandwiches. We watched as London, busy as always, passed by, and eventually we slipped out of the Thames Estuary and into the sea, and there was a great cheer.

"Will we be safe in the boat?" Duffy asked when the boat rocked a bit. "I do hope so," I said, and Colin cooed, ruffling his hair, "Don't worry if it capsizes. I will be Jack and you, my Rose." And everyone laughed.

Outside, the wind and waves lashed the boat, and it tipped and lurched. Regina looked positively green and alternated between holding onto Fiona. Fiona patted her hand, "Goodness, how much longer will this journey be?"

Archie shrugged, "Dad said it's around five hours."

"Five hours!" Regina said in a heated, queasy voice, "Surely there are less ridiculous ways of getting to the island. Why on earth are we doing this ridiculous voyage?"

"Tradition," I said, smiling. Regina's sorry state was amusing at first, but as the hours whittled on, the laughter died out as we all found that the endless listing and lurching of the boat was getting to us. I was rather enjoying the voyage before that; the English coastline was ever so charming, and watching the cliffs and cities slip by was quite lovely. Sir Hugh, who alone seemed unstirred by the endless spinning of the sea, spent the voyage regaling us with the academy's history.

He said that when the holy twins first set sail, they were besieged by a great storm and St Bartholomew stayed on deck wrestling with the sheet and sail while his sister retreated down below deck to pray for the storm to still. And apparently it did with clouds giving way to sunshine. I had suggested Regina start praying, and she gave me a very unamused green glare.

By the end of the voyage, all conversation and games of shuffleboard had long since died out, and everyone was sitting in silence, holding their stomachs and trying very hard not to get sick all over.

Finally, when all hope of seeing land again seemed bleak, out of eddying rain and mist loomed the island. An immense rock, as jagged as glass, and atop it was a sprawling castle reaching out from the green and grey. It was more like a small maze of castles, a claw grasping up for heaven.

"There she is," called Sir Hugh, and despite the stinging whip of the rain, we'd all stepped on to the deck watching as the castle and the island loomed closer. Suddenly, it was above, blocking off the rain. I stared, mesmerised at the sheer immensity of it all. Sir Hugh led us in procession up the beach and through a path through the small forest where the trees grew thick and tall on either side. They bore an uncanny resemblance to the woods back home, having the same rather ancient, gnarled sort of look. I know for a fact that the Whistling Woods are indeed what remains of an ancient forest. I wondered if it was the same for the trees at the academy, and if the two forests had been connected in an ancient, primordial world? The castle grew closer and closer, and soon it was upon us. I remembered how many generations of Rooks had been here before me, and that I had sipped onto another part of an ancient legacy.

The island and the castle resembled a rather spider-like and labyrinthine beast. I loved it immediately, and I love it still.

Soon, we came before a massive cathedral-like building that seemed to be a twin to the Rolling Rock. Sir Hugh led us up the grand staircase to a chapel. It's called The Great Chapel or The Chapel of St Bartholomew and is apparently where St Bartholomew first knelt in prayer upon docking on the island. We all sat down in a disassembled, random way whilst Sir Hugh climbed onto a podium.

"Welcome, welcome to the academy. Welcome home!" he said with a deep smile, and there was tremendously loud whooping and applauding.

Sir Hugh let us have a moment before he spoke up, "This is both a joyous and solemn moment. You are no longer children. You are now young men and women. You are no longer coddled and protected. We are your teachers…"

He paused, gesturing at the robed figures standing on the periphery, who had remained silent. "We will be both compassionate and firm, as we carry you all higher into wonderful strata of education."

I didn't hear the rest because Archie groaned, "Oh, this is it. This is what's going to kill me." And I tried hard to stifle a chuckle.

"And of course," finished Sir Hugh jokingly, "there will be plenty of time for sports." He paused to allow for another raucous round of cheering and excited conversation. "Now. Time for bed, but first you will all stand up, shake each other's hands, and once you finish, you will cross the floor and shake hands with your teachers."

Once we were done, the prefects came to take us to our dorms. The nervous thrill of excitement carried on in whispers of excited conversation as we stepped out into the rain. There were two prefects, one for the boys and one for the girls. Electra Barking was the prefect for the girls, which didn't surprise me as, in addition to being beautiful and athletically gifted, she was extraordinarily level-headed in sharp contrast to her brother.

The male prefect was my godmother Rosemary's son, Scholar. Which was rather ironic, but I assume he had either sobered up considerably or was somehow able to trick the school into thinking him more trustworthy than he actually was. He abandoned his post at the head of the line and came over, "Hey Hammy," he said, looking down at me and ruffling my hair. He leaned in close and whispered.

"Oh, you'd better rest up well tonight. You have a very early start tomorrow." And he sauntered off without elaborating.

Duffy sighed, "I suspect that will be the student-led initiation.

"I know," I said, grinning broadly, "I can't wait."

The first-year dormitory, called the Twins, was a rather odd structure consisting of two identical towers with a common area connecting the two. The boys and girls were in separate towers, with the girls tower called the Maiden's tower, and the boys tower called Bachelor's tower. We parted ways with laughter, exaggerated farewells, and the sort of crude jokes that only nervous teenagers away from home for the first time could muster.

Colin and I were particularly thrilled to discover that our room was on the very top floor, though the realisation came with the sobering acknowledgement that we'd have to haul ourselves – and our luggage – up an exhausting number of stairs.

We got there a bit winded from the exertion and excitement, and Colin excitedly fumbled with the key as he opened our room for the first time.

I was about to step in, but he stopped me and picked me up bridal style. "Colin," I gasped, wrapping my arms around him to steady myself, "What on earth are you doing?"

He grinned down at me, "Well, it's tradition, isn't it? To be carried over the threshold?"

I rolled my eyes, not able to force down my smile or the heat crawling up my cheeks, "I think that only applies to newlyweds, you big oaf, but I suppose I can allow it this once."

"Thought so," he said with a victorious smirk as he pushed the door open, stepping over the threshold with exaggerated ceremony "Besides, I think it suits us, don't you?" he said as he tossed me on the bed before turning to survey the room

I was rather impressed. It was as large (almost) as my room back home. A high ceiling with three windows which overlooked the spitting silver sea on one side, and a good bit of the island on the other.

There was just one tiny problem, which was that there were not two, but three beds and three desks. I was rather confused, as on the form we filled out, Colin and I had specifically requested a two-person room. The lads had stayed up till midnight the night the forms opened, just to ensure we'd have first pick.

"Scholar," Colin called, and Scholar jogged over. "Why are there three beds? It's supposed to be just me and Hamlet—"

Scholar frowned, "Your parents did tell you about the third roommate?"

"We specifically requested a double," I protested, and Scholar shrugged, "Sorry your parents had a very specific request."

I had a horrible sinking feeling in my stomach and a rather terrifying prediction of just who that third roommate might be.

"Well…" Colin asked, "Who is this third roommate?"

And woe to heaven, my prediction proved true for Nicholas Barking strolled over, looking deeply unhappy. I need not say that sharing a room or any form of close quarters with Nicholas Barking wasn't quite something on my bucket list, especially since I knew him to be a murderer! Nor was I entirely confident in the power of that nasty secret he, Regina and I shared because on further reflection it gave him a reason to want me dead (not that he was pleased with me being alive regardless)

I am quite confident that I could break him like a twig in a fair fight, but should he come down upon me when I was sleeping, I would probably not be able to put up much of a fight. I didn't, of course, say any of these things to Scholar.

But Scholar merely shrugged, told us it wasn't up to him and ushered us inside and told us to get ready for lights out, and walked away, ignoring Colin's swearing.

"I am very sorry about your mother, Barking. But why are you doing this to us?" Colin snapped to Nicholas, who scowled, "I don't want this either. I had requested a single. I do not like either of you very much. As I have made clear over the years."

"Oh," I demanded, "So, this just happened of its own accord then? Perhaps the gods of fate decided to have some fun at my expense and saddle me with you!?"

He rolled his eyes, "No, not a god of fate… a god of spite. My dear dad is always harping on about us getting on. I suppose this was all his meddling… believe me, Rook, I would rather sleep out in the cold than in here with you and your friend."

I was about to suggest he do just that, but I was exhausted and a bit peckish and sensing the futility of the conversation, I decided to table my anger till the morning.

Nicholas grabbed his pyjamas and miscellaneous shower items and stormed out. When he left, Colin was still fuming, but I assured him it would be alright and that we could still do all the things we planned to do as roommates, such as movie nights and simply ignore Nicholas. Colin eventually calmed down.

There was a great deal of exchanged whispers in the hallway as people went back and forth from the showers. The bathrooms themselves were somehow both plush and spartan, with gleaming tiles and just enough austerity to remind us that this was an academy, not a hotel.

I laughed off warnings about the water being cold, waited a while, and just hopped in. I screamed when the rather stygian spray hit me, and a lot of laughing followed. I took a short shower, dressed and ran shivering back to my bed and hopped under my deep green sheets. It had been a long day, and before long, I was sinking into the land of dreams.

Chapter Twenty-One

The next morning (if so pale an hour can be called that), I woke up to someone shoving a wet sock in my face. The sock wielder in question was Theo Marlow-Saint Clair, a senior on the football team. He held a finger to his lips, shushed me and gestured for us to follow him.

Still bleary from my rather rude awakening, I followed an equally bemused Colin and a silently venomous Nicholas. Out in the hallway, the other boys in our year were all gathered, looking utterly groggy and confused. Archie, in particular, looked out of sorts, wearing only his boxers and looking utterly comical next to Duffy, wearing his car's pyjamas.

"Okay, St Claire, what is the meaning of this?" Archie had snapped, but in answer, Marlow-St Claire held a silent finger to his lips.

The girls had been roused too and were being led down by Windsor's sister, the Princess Georgina and with their hair undone and their faces unmade, they looked as ill rested as we did. Together we filed out into the morning's cold, and Duffy protested being made to walk around in the rather mercurial temperatures in just our pyjamas (or boxers in Archie's case).

We followed Georgina and Theo, and they led us down a winding path away from the building and through the trees. Hooded figures loomed out of the darkness of the trees, some wielding flaming torches, all wearing these odd silver masks.

No one dared utter a whisper, though there were many confused and questioning looks passed around. And dear sweet Duffy had squeezed himself in between Archie and me in an attempt to keep himself out of the view of the silent sentinels.

Their eyes followed us as we silently walked down to the beach; the sea and sky were dark and still, and the pebble beach crunched underfoot. We were led to the water's edge, and the sweet smell of the sea peppered us with frigid kisses.

"Good morning, you handsome boys and beautiful girls," called Jago Stormwater- Keyne, a tall, handsome lad of eighteen, with sandy blond hair, blue eyes and a Ralph Lauren smile.

He shushed the grumbling, "Now, boys and girls, if you wanna make it at this storied school of ours, you must earn our respect and grumbling about being made to wake up early from your beauty sleep is quite the bad first impression for you. Especially as we all awoke hours earlier, just so that we could greet you. So don't be so vocal with your ingratitude." When everyone quieted, he smiled and turned towards the sea.

The sea was lazy, slow and calm. It was even darker out there than it had been on the green, the rising sun being hidden by the island behind us. "Do you hear that?" he asked, and after much whispering, we fell silent to listen. Sure enough, over the sounds of shore and sea, we could hear the chime of a bell, earnest and clear.

"That's the Inchscape bell," Jago said, "It was hung by some ancient abbot aeons ago so as to alert sailors of the dangers of the cliffs." He smiled out at the still sea, "Legend has it he still rings it! It's out on a buoy in the sea about a quarter of a mile or so. And now you are probably wondering why I am telling you all this."

He smiled amicably, patting Duffy on his back, "One of you has the honour of swimming out there bringing it back here. And because we are not heartless dicks, another person will take it back out and restore it," he said casually, "One boy and one girl. And before you protest, if two people don't volunteer, then all of you shall be punished. And yes, you are being hazed. Going once."

Everyone was eager to prove themselves, so several people volunteered, but my hand hit the air first. Jago grinned, "Ah, Rook, perfect… now one for the girls."

Several hands hit the air. Jago considered for a moment, "Lady Regina, thank you very much. He gestured at us with his hands, "Now, how about a cheer for cur tributes?" And the resounding cheers echoed off the sounding sea.

"Alright, Rook, you're first up," Jago said.

And I thought I was being rather brave as I charged into the water. I figured it would make it easier, but boy, was I wrong. I felt as though a great ice hand had slapped me, and I almost screamed. And I had half a mind to flee out of the water and beg someone else to take my place.

But a Rook never surrenders, and behind me, my friends cheered me on. And so I began to swim in the vague direction of the bell. Every inch of my body felt like it was being impaled by icy needles. I normally adored swimming in the sea, but that was during the day and in warmer climes. The sea in the darkness before dawn is a different beast, and though from the shore the water seemed still and calm, it was far from it. I was punched and tossed around. My normally perfect form failed, and I pawed, clawed and scratched wildly at the water. Finally, I came within sight of a buoy with a bell tied to it. I was upon it, and I climbed, almost screaming out of the hellishly cold water.

I clung to the buoy, which carried a cold of its own, and I just hung there for a moment. My muscles seemed to have aged a few decades, and I couldn't have parted from my embrace with the buoy if I wanted to.

With numb fingers, I managed to untie the bell and grasped it as tight as I could back into the icy waters. I fought against the freezing water and finally reached land. I stood up, clutching onto the bell and staggered stiffly to the shore. I realised I was crying, but mercifully so soaked was I, that no one could tell. I was welcomed to the beach with a resounding cheer. I handed the bell to Jago and dropped onto the sand. He patted my hair. "Rook might be short, but he is stout of heart," he said, hoisting the bell. "Get the poor boy to the fire, someone."

The others applauded me, and I was wrapped in many hugs. And then I ran over to the side, and I threw up. A few laughed, and others clapped me on the back. Colin came over, gently leading me over to a bonfire they had built on the beach, and I dropped beside it. I watched dully as Regina took the bell from Jago to a great cheer and dove into the water.

As we watched her swim further and further out, the group fell into solemn, almost reverent, church-like silence. And the only sound was the whisper of the sea and the crackling of the driftwood. She was back, stepping out of the water like a hypothermic Aphrodite and looking rather like she'd seen the devil. Her red hair fell damp around her; her skin was pale.

The hooded figures ran onto the beach shouting and cheering. Jago clapped, "Welcome to the academy, ladies and gents."

Another cheer echoed off the sea. I was having the absolute time of my life.

After that, we flocked to the grand dining hall for breakfast (there was sausage, eggs, toast, kippers and various juices). Then we were assembled on the quad and led around the island on a tour. It struck me just how large the island was. It had space for the school buildings, the dorms, several sports fields and still had room for several acres of dense woodland. Once the tour was over, we were free for the rest of the day.

Regina had grown quite entranced with the library and wanted to explore it in more detail. The library, I had to admit, was almost breathtaking in its sheer grandeur. I strolled around the library, which had been neatly divided into sections based on subject matter. There was, of course, an entire wing dedicated to languages. Then the usual… geography, chemistry, biology, geology and the like and then it splintered into subjects like sociology and anthropology and such, which had multiple shelves devoted to each subject.

And then, at the very end, up against the windows, was an occult section. It sat in a large, deep alcove, rather weirdly divorced from the rest of the library; the books were dusty and seldom touched. I took one off the shelves, and it sent dust mites spinning and glinting in the sunlight. It was quiet there, the books long since untouched, almost like people were afraid to stray there, too frightened by warnings at Sunday school or whatever. Right across it was a rather nice spot; there were desk chairs, armchairs and large windows that overlooked the sea.

After that, we all had lunch, and Duffy and I went over to the field where the rest of the polo team had been waiting on the green. It was a small team, far smaller than any of the other school teams.

Bartholomew Abernathy-Heath, who was the captain, jovially greeted us when we walked onto the field. "Hello chaps," he said, "Welcome to your first practice."

Duffy and I were very excited and very eager to start drills, warm up and the like. But Electra made an amused tittering noise. "Now, no, not so fast. There is a little tradition you must partake in first." This mercifully was merely a ride around the obstacle course and not another plunge into the sea. Granny had gotten me a new horse, a splendid chestnut stallion, which I wasn't quite sure what to name. My old childhood horse, Chocolate, died two years ago. He had been a sweet, gentle thing, unlike this one, who had a sprite-ish spirit. Anyway, he let me saddle him long enough to ride around the island, and only threw me off once.

When we were all done, Barnaby called us into a circle, "You know fellows, I had rather a rotten end of my ear. Lily broke up with me in December. And I tell you, the 7th of December shall go down in history as one of the saddest days since Bloody Saturday."

Electra frowned "Barney… do you even know what Bloody Saturday is?"

"No. Anyway," he went on, "Welcome to the sport of kings!" *Cheer! Cheer! Cheer!*

Chapter Twenty-Two

The year commenced, and some of my classes were a trifle more exciting, especially the biology classroom, which had shelves with all manner of skeletons and bugs in jars. Business and finance did promise some interest. I think I shall do best at those two. I love biology, and we Rooks do have a natural affinity for business.

The only vaguely exciting thing was when I punched Nicholas Barking, but I can't even count it as satisfying because I got detention for it.

Well, it all started in English Literature, which, of course, is taught by Sir Hugh. We had been tasked with reading Julius Caesar over the winter holiday, but I had rather forgotten about it.

Sir Hugh was trying valiantly to shepherd us through a discussion, though with rather mixed results. There was genuine enthusiasm from the usual eager souls, but the rest of the room had sunk into a languid haze of collective distraction. Colin and I were having a very polite, very quiet, whispered conversation in our corner; our whispers were not disrupting or disturbing anyone else.

But Sir Hugh had had enough, and he strolled over with, "Well, I see there is quite a lively discussion taking place in this corner," his voice dripping with reproach. "Would either of you young gentlemen care to enlighten the class with your thoughts on Brutus' suicide?"

The class turned in unison, their collective gaze turning to us with mingled amusement and some with satisfaction.

I sighed and rose, because what else could one do under such scrutiny? "Well," I began, stalling for time, "suicide is… um…"

Colin, ever helpful, had only nodded encouragingly, though he didn't contribute on his own.

"Well, suicide is sort of cowardly, isn't it?" I said finally. "Brutus does it to avoid… um, the consequences of his treason."

Sir Hugh exhaled audibly, a sound that managed to combine disappointment, weariness, and mild disdain into one efficient sigh. "Yes, Lord Rook, that is perhaps a reading of the text," he said, his tone growing sharp. "But I would suggest it's not the most sensitive thing to say, and perhaps not the best way to approach the matter."

He turned to walk away, leaving me standing under the weight of the class's collective attention. Most moved on in a few moments, but not Nicholas Barking. Nicholas had been sitting directly in front of me, silent and stiff, his gaze unnervingly cold.

He said nothing then, but as soon as the class ended, he was waiting for me. I barely made it out the door before he grabbed my shoulder and yanked me around to face him. His face was close to mine, his expression tight and furious.

"So, Rook," he hissed, his voice low and dangerous, "tell me more about how suicide is cowardly."

I shrugged, trying for nonchalance. "Well, it's the easiest option, isn't it? Brutus didn't want to face the consequences of his actions. The right thing to do would've been to surrender himself to Antonio's forces and accept his punishment. Instead, he took the path of least resistance. Cowardly."

Nicholas stared at me, his expression hardening with every word. Then, without warning, he punched me.

"You son of a whore!" he spat. "My mother wasn't a coward!"

The room, which had been loud with post-class chatter, fell instantly silent. His punch didn't hurt, not really – Nicholas was all wiry limbs and no muscle to speak of. What caught me off guard was the sheer audacity of it.

So, I punched him back. Not hard, mind you, I was considerate of his haemophilia. But hard enough to get my point across.

Nicholas recoiled, his face a storm of fury and humiliation, and lunged at me with all his customary ineffective rage. Sir Hugh, who had been calling for order in vain, finally reached us. He grabbed us both by the shoulders, his grip impressively firm for a man his age, and marched us out of the room.

Sir Hugh took me to his office, while Nicholas was off to the nurse (unnecessarily if you ask me). I sat down in a rather stiff-backed armchair as he surveyed me over his glasses with the air of a disappointed grandfather, "Hamlet, do take a seat."

I mutely obeyed, and he went on, "I must tell you I am extremely disappointed. Over the break, I had the impression you were a bright if spirited boy, but here you are getting into fights in the first week. I..."

"Please call me Lord Hamlet, Sir," I interrupted, "I prefer only my friends call me Hamlet, and I apologise, but Nicholas Barking did start it. He threw the first slap."

Sir Hugh was silent for a moment, "Yes, sorry... *Lord* Hamlet. Now, I know Nicholas Barking has had his fair share of behavioural issues, and yes, he did throw the first punch, but—"

"There we go," I said, "You admit he punched me, unprovoked. That, I think, should free me from any and all blame in this 'particular instance'. Don't you agree, sir?"

His intense, rain grey eyes were boring holes into me, how I hated those eyes and his stupid, all-knowing face. "Do you truly believe that? That he struck you 'unprovoked' as you said?"

"Yes."

Sir Hugh leaned forward the fraction of an inch, "Alright. Lord Hamlet, do you remember what you said in class? Or what you were saying to his face before he slapped you?"

I faltered for a moment, "Well. We were talking about Julius Caesar, and we were discussing Brutus's suicide. And I said that he was a coward as he took the easy way out and escaped the consequences for his treason."

Sir Hugh's eyes still hadn't left me, and I dropped my gaze to the ground, "But that is not all that you said, is it? You made an insensitive comment on a rather delicate topic. Is that not true? By calling Brutus a coward, you also insulted those who may have dealt with suicidal thoughts or have experienced losing someone to suicide. Don't you agree?"

I felt a bite of sickening shame. "Well, no… and what does that have to do with Nicholas?" I asked, "What I said was not remotely directed at him. I do not understand why he took offence at it."

Sir Hugh sat back and was silent for a moment, his fingers tapping at the desk, "Do you truly not know the reason why he might take offence? Or did you know the history and yet said it just to hurt him… in which case…."

I felt another sharp twist of anger, "Sir, I apologise, but are you going to pose me riddles all day?

Sir Hugh gave a dry little chuckle, "I'll just cut to the chase…. Lady Barking took her own life." I felt a rather intense horror at myself, and I rather wished that a ceiling light had taken me out in class. I had thought it was ail a rumour, "Oh."

Sir Hugh smiled gently, "Let me ask you… had you known about the horrid circumstances behind his mother's death, would you have said the same thing about Brutus being a coward?"

My tea had gone room temperature and was rather pale, so I set it back down on the desk. "Of course not."

Sir Hugh smiled fully, "I thought not. Now, Lord Hamlet, tell me… why did you feel the need to punch him back?"

I looked him in the eyes again, "I often find violence is the only way to deal with violence."

Sir Hugh sighed, "Yes, you have made that clear, but you have to understand that at the end of the day, he was acting out of grief and frustration. I am not saying it excuses him from attacking you, but humans are humans. And a little empathy never hurts."

Sir," I said, failing to keep the anger from my tone, "Unless you yourself are without flaw, and have never acted out in anger, are you really in any position to judge me?"

His smile faltered by a fraction, "I have, and I won't deny my own past. But believe me… I am speaking from a long life of experience. You don't want to be like me." His gaze dropped momentarily to the floor, but then returned to my face.

There was a moment of lingering silence, and then I asked, "Why aren't you talking to Barking? He did throw the first punch regardless of what I said."

Sir Hugh frowned. "Whether I talk to Lord Nicholas is beside the point. Right now, I am talking to you – a young man who needs guidance, and who has yet to learn basic principles such as self-control."

I couldn't hide my scowl at this, "And why might that be? Is it because Nicholas is white, and I am not?" Of course, I knew that wasn't the case, but I was upset, and I wanted to get a rise out of Sir Drinkwater.

He was silent for the count of five. "Is that what you really believe, that I am discriminating against you on the basis of race?"

I shrugged, "I merely find the discrepancy fascinating. He threw the first punch, and I take full responsibility for what I said, but he could have resolved it with words, couldn't he? The only difference between Nicholas and me is that he is white and that I am part Indian."

Sir Hugh gaped at me, "You seem like an intelligent boy, but sometimes you are too quick to draw wrong conclusions. Oh, and for the record, it doesn't matter to me whether you are Indian or white, male or female, gay or straight. What matters to me is the kind of person you are."

He went silent again, his mouth twisting into an unhappy moue, "Tell me… why did you hit him back? Was it just pettiness or cruelty? You don't strike me as a cruel boy, Lord Rook. Rash and arrogant, yes, but not a sadist."

"Well," I said, "You, the school and his mother let him run roughshod over everyone, and there's always an excuse, whether it's his dead mother or his haemophilia. I punched him back because I knew that was the only justice I'd see."

He scoffed, "So, a slap for a slap. You know what they say about the whole world being blind."

"Then we shall be blind together. Seems a fair world to me, Sir," I said, "Would you rather he had gotten away unpunished?"

Sir Hugh seemed to struggle for a moment, "Lord Hamlet, you are a good lad, and I have faith in you, and I want to try and help you and

Nicholas. Both. He has never learned how to get along with people or make friends. And this is why I must come up with a different approach with him... you two will be serving detention together."

I sputtered for a few moments, "What? Why?"

Sir Hugh seemed vaguely amused, "Nicholas and you will have to serve detention together, it is only appropriate since you both took part in the fight. I thought that's what you wanted?"

"But why can't we serve separately… he can sit here with you, and I can run laps or something."

Sir Hugh sighed, "Because you two have a long history of animosity. Might I ask when this started?"

I sighed with a shrug, "I honestly don't know... he's never liked me, even when we were children."

He nodded, "Lord Hamlet, tell me, have you ever tried talking to him? Not all problems are solved with violence. If you give it a chance, I think you will find that your hatred can give way to empathy."

I sighed, "Sir, as sweet as that might be, unfortunately, Nicholas Barking is incapable of being civil. Besides, I do not wish to have a conversation with a person who has spent years picking on me."

He sighed, "You seem to think this is a choice I am giving you. You and Nicholas will be serving detention together, and with a spot of luck, that will give way to conversation, reluctant or not."

I set down my teacup so hard it splashed onto his desk, "Now that's not fair!"

"Lord Hamlet," he said, raising his voice for the first time, "I am your headmaster, and this matter is not up for debate."

I made to protest, but Sir Hugh held up a hand again, "Forget about Nicholas. Lord Hamlet, you're a gifted student, a talented sportsman, you have a good group of friends, you are charming, good-looking and come from a great lineage."

"Sir, are you scolding me or proposing to me?" I asked, "And I don't see how spending my lunch reading Shakespeare with you and him will change anything."

Sir Hugh sighed, "I am sure you won't admit it, but you two are two peas in a pod, and as much as you hate each other, you are in a way the same. The first step we need is to help you two learn how not to let your tempers and pride take control of you. And as for the Shakespeare readings, I misspoke. We won't just be reading Shakespeare, but several very great writers. Literature, you will find, if you give it the chance, is the story of the human heart."

I sighed, "I guess I don't have a choice, do I, Sir?"

"You do not," he said cheerfully, "You must understand that the way you two express your anger is unhealthy, it must be dealt with in some way. If we can help you two learn how to control that aspect, it is possible you might one day learn to forgive each other. Until then, I ask that you and Nicholas be civil to each other in my presence."

"I will if he will," I said quietly.

He smiled again, "That is a start. And your mother asks you to call her and please, on your way out, send Nicholas in, will you?"

Chapter Twenty-Three

Whenever I find myself overwrought or frustrated, I like to step among the trees. I like to close my eyes and listen to the leaves, to the earth, and feel the endless dance of creation and let the soil bury my frustrations and turmoil. Did you know that in old forests, there exists a sort of fungal network that stretches between the roots and the boughs? It's an incredibly complex organism, and in many ways, it is quite literally the forest talking. It's been here since the first trees and is, to me, the truest form of magic there is.

I remembered the woods back at Rook Manor; the trees there were just as old and thick. It almost seemed like these two forests, separated by miles of land and sea, might have been fitted together in an ancient world. As a boy, I was often plagued by odd dreams and poor sleep. So on my more restless nights, I'd slip from my bed with Baskerville and my trusty stuffed dragon. I'd made a game of sneaking to the tree line and waiting… staring into the darkness and waiting for the sun to rise. However, in fear, I'd bolt back into the house, with a child's dogmatic certainty that the devil was chasing me. I could almost feel… almost see his hands burned and red, grabbing and groping for me.

He never caught me. I always made it back to the house in time, but he did catch me in dreams, and I'd awake wailing and shrieking. Mother would try to comfort me, assuring me it was nothing more than dreams. But it was Granny who eased my fears. She'd sat on my bed, gently rubbing my back.

"Never fear the dark, child. There is nothing there that is not in the light. Never fear the woods; the devil is not in the woods. The tempter cannot abide there; the smell of trees and the sounds of birds remind him of what he has forfeited. The woods are your friend."

It's odd, really. Granny never left the manor, preferring her needlework and tending her garden. Grandpa and Mother used to judge her for it. She was a Lady and ex-Prime Minister's wife after all, why did she not do more with her life? But I always found she had a calmness and wisdom that they lacked.

From then on, instead of running away, I went into the woods when I couldn't sleep. I'd sit on a fallen bough, clutching the dragon while Baskerville curled at my feet. I'd listen to the singing crickets and the rustle of the wind through the trees until I sometimes fell asleep there. The woods, as Granny said, were my friend.

Years later, they still gave me peace, but just then, for a moment, it seemed a man woven of tree and sunlight watched me. The moment I turned to him, he disappeared. I leaned back and basked in the sun through the trees. I wanted that moment to last forever, but I'd promised Colin I'd support him at his first rugby practice, and so I made my way back over to the campus.

I walked alone. Just me and the sea and the trees, or so I had thought until there were hurried footsteps. And suddenly I was viscerally reminded of a body in the snow… a face out of the darkness and something being swung at me.

I gave a startled cry and raised my hands. And there was a surprised laugh. Electra Barking stood there, "Goodness, Rook," she said, "Did I startle you?"

"Sorry," I muttered, waiting for my heart to stop playing the hare, "Just a bit on edge. You know the excitement of the new… of starting at the academy. And well…"

"That woman being murdered at your mother's Christmas party?" She provided a slightly sardonic smile.

I nodded mutely. Her blue eyes flashed, "Oh, I have been meaning to ask. Did you see anything untoward that night?"

"Well, I did get attacked by someone. And I thought I caught a glimpse of a pale face. I think it was…. I don't know, actually." I remembered that pale face I had seen disappearing into the storm. I had been utterly convinced it was Nicholas, but if Regina insisted, then maybe I was wrong.

She laughed and prodded my nose, "Well… could the person who attacked you have been my brother?"

I fell silent, remembering the pale face. Suddenly, the blur of the face seemed to morph into the sneering face of Nicholas. I did not respond, and Electra took me by the arm "So," she asked cheerfully, "Where are you off to?"

"Um... the rugby field… I promised Colin I would come watch his first practice. But I think I am a bit lost."

She smiled, offering an elbow, and I, with a blush, interlocked our elbows. And she led me on the way.

"You see, my darling brother has been odd since that dull woman died. Don't get me wrong. He has always been an odd child, but since that night, he's become even more withdrawn," she said earnestly, "I know you and Regina were lying when you alibied him that night."

"You know about that?" I asked.

"Oh yes," said in a voice of soft amusement, "My father told me all about it. He is so very proud. He was rather worried…"

"About what?"

"Well, let's just say my brother has had his fair share of admirers. Girls your age love that dark, brooding type. But he's never shown much interest in any of them," she said. I sighed internally. Yes, a lot of girls fancied him. I always found it ludicrous.

"My father always worried about Nicholas… didn't have any interest in matters of the heart. He was afraid Nicholas would die alone, an old bachelor taking the family name with him. So, the old man was quite relieved to see his son dating such a lovely young lady."

She shrugged, seeming amused at some secret jest and went on. "But, I for one think he's more interested in books than girls or boys… so I have no doubt that there is nothing beyond conspiracy between him and Lady Regina… and you."

I swallowed, "Well…"

She didn't let me finish, and she went on, "And lest you forget, Nicholas knows you know his secret. And you know best of all how dangerous he is. Just imagine what he might do to keep his secret..."

I had wanted to say that I could take him, and in truth, I probably could, but Nicholas was sly and cunning, and good at pretending to be innocent. He could find a way to… kill me and make it look like an accident.

I swallowed, unsure of what to say, and she wrapped herself around me and walked up the path.

I came upon the rugby field, and Colin stood out from all the others because not only was he quite a bit taller, but his bright red hair stood out like a flare. He came bounding up to me. He was rather bruised and very ruddy, but looking like he was having the time of his life.

"You look like you're having fun," I said, and he nodded rather bouncily. "Oh, I do. I get to tackle so many people," he said breathlessly.

"You like tackling people?"

"I do," he had begun, and then I tackled him. Or well attempted to, he is after all quite a bit larger than me, but all l I managed to do was make him stumble back a bit. "Oh, you little twat," he laughed, and we wrestled back and forth till Jago Keyne (also captain of the boys' rugby team) came and sent Colin back over to the drills.

"You know our friend Duffy is mighty upset with me about that hazing thing," he said.

"Oh, you can expect his forgiveness on judgment day," I said, and he laughed, "So, Hamsta," he said, draping an arm around me, "Whatcha doing tonight?"

"Well, Colin and I are going to rewatch the *Lord of the Rings* trilogy."

"Aw. Come on, Rook," Jago said, "Don't tell me you'd rather spend time with De Winter than with me."

I stared at him blankly, "Well, I hate to say this, but I would. No offence though, Keyne."

"Oh," and pouted with a hand over his heart, "Well, I am offended. You are hurting my feelings, Hamsta," he said and then with a faux sigh, "Alright, once you and Clifford the big red dog are finished with your movie, do you wanna meet me in the old clearing?"

"Oh, alright," I said and, smirking, he ruffled my hair and ran off back to practice.

Evening came with a cool sea breeze and the singing of crickets. I'd carried the tension of the day in my shoulders and in the bones of my skull. But as the sky turned purple, and the sounds of laughter and whistling tree leaves filled the air, I felt it all ebb away. I closed my eyes and leaned my face towards the dying sunshine.

I was almost able to forget Hugh and the looming shadow of Nicholas Barking.

I say almost because my little moment of tranquillity was shattered when I opened my eyes and saw Nicholas Barking up above me, staring down from the tower window.

When he saw me looking, he slipped back and out of sight, and I felt a prickle of unease. I can't quite explain. I felt like he'd been watching me specifically, as though waiting. … Before I could do anything, however, Regina sauntered over in her field hockey kit, "How was practice?" I asked. Her face was aglow from the exercise, and she smiled, "I think I did rather well. Bede Longfellow said, " If I keep it up, I might make captain.

"No surprise there, of course," I said.

A pebble fell off the castle roof and rolled out in front of us. Jago frowned at it and then looked up. Suddenly, above me, there was a great crack, and I looked up in time to see the face of a gargoyle bearing down on me. Jago grabbed and spun us both out of the way, and there was a deafening, almighty crash as the stone gargoyle exploded against the spot where I had just been standing. I spent a long moment clinging to Jago, and I couldn't hear very much over the screaming in my ears.

Colin came running over, "Bloody hell?" I looked at him, and I realised I was shaking. He looked at me and then up at the roof, "How the hell did that fall?"

I realised I was still clinging to Jago, and I pried myself off him. (Regina, if you're at this part, shut up.) There was a great deal of commotion and a lot of noise. James, St James appeared, "I heard the sound! What on earth happened?"

Regina was gripping my hand very tightly, and Jago, who was still standing very close to me, muttered, "Practice dismissed."

Colin insisted I go to the school's nurse when Duffy ran up, followed by Fiona and Polly.

Polly slapped me on the shoulder, "We heard about your near-death experience. Sounds wicked."

Fiona was rather upset, "Goodness, imagine that gargoyle was perfectly fixed up there for centuries… they really should be taking better care of these old structures."

Regina frowned, "Fiona does have a point, it certainly is quite odd that that gargoyle, after centuries of loyally guarding the castle, should choose that exact moment to fall, especially with seemingly nothing to bring about its collapse."

I remembered a pale face disappearing above me, and I remembered a dancing shadow after the ugly bust fell. Regina was right. That statue hadn't fallen on its own.

Nicholas had pushed it.

Chapter Twenty-Four

Everything Nicholas did… every breath, every gesture, no matter how innocuous, seemed to me to be a taunt. Of course with him in my room, in my classes and on my island, it was impossible to escape him. That Friday night, Regina and I went for a walk. The sun stayed up late, and the winds were warm. We walked onto the beach, walking by the spinning, sounding sea "Goodness," Regina had said, "What a week."'

It had been a long, slightly tiring week, but rather exhilarating. My favourite class by far was PE. Of course, the general dreariness of February in the North Sea meant class was held in the school's weight room. I normally do not enjoy indoor days, but the games mistress (Mrs Radcliffe) had moved into a segment on free-weight exercises, which I found rather fun. Before long, it became something of a competition between the boys to see who could do the most push-ups or pull-ups. Unsurprisingly, Colin, being the tallest and the biggest, was able to by far outperform the rest.

Nicholas Barking did not enjoy these days and struggled to do even a single pull-up, but contented himself to walk idly on the treadmill.

The detentions had been going well, in that Nicholas and I weren't fighting, but I hated every moment I had to spend with the ever-smiling Sir Hugh and the ever-sullen Nicholas Barking. I decided that I hated them both, and I hated Shakespeare. Although Shakespeare at least was funny.

Despite Duffy's whining, football practices were actually a pretty bracing way to start the day. We started with a jog around the beach and then jogged over to the field, where we did stretches and played two games as practice. It was always greatly enjoyable, even on the more arctic days. And usually, the girls were let out early and so came to spectate and cheer us on. We spent the first two days (Monday and Wednesday) simply doing drills, doing some riding practice and learning about hooks and knock-ins, but on Friday, we had the actual games, which were a lot more chaotic than I had anticipated but utterly fun!

"What a week indeed," I said.

I nodded, "Do…you think it's all connected? The flowers… Lady Moira?"

Regina's fingers toyed with the pebbles of the beach, and she was silent for a moment, "Well… it all seems to be, doesn't it? Think about it, darling, the flowers arrived the same day Moira Barking died… this all seems to have started with her death."

I looked out at the sea, which, even with the wind, was still as silver glass. "Do you remember the conversation we'd overheard that night? They talked about all the odd things that have been happening… Lady Barking's death, Mr Singh's accident, and Dahlia's death… I think you're right… It's all connected somehow."

Her red hair danced in the breeze, and she stared out at the sea. Regina's eyes were a strange and beautiful thing that seemed to shift colour depending on the light; one moment they were blue as robin's eggs, the next the green of the forest. And as we stood there watching the sluggish sea, her eyes were a pale blueish grey, almost the precise colour of the sea. "I am inclined to agree. But of course, none of our parents will tell us…so we must find the answers ourselves."

I sighed, picking at the crest ring around my finger. I had grown quite accustomed to the weight, and it made an excellent fidgeting device when I was bored.

We stood there glorying in our shared purpose. We imagined ourselves as great detectives to rival Holmes and the little French fellow.

And suddenly there was the sound of a twig or branch snapping behind us. So silent were the wind and sea, that it had been like a gunshot. Regina and I whipped around, but there was nothing but shadows and stillness. I turned back to the sea, "Alright then, Watson."

But Regina's fingernails dug into my shoulder, "Let's go." Her eyes were still focused on the shadows of the treeline, and her face was pale.

I obeyed, and we walked quickly and quietly back to the cheery glow of the lit pathway.

We kept a rather brisk pace until we were back in the dorms. And only then did we relax. Regina laughed, "Well," she said, "I for one desperately need a bath. Goodnight darling. Oh, and darling? If anything, I am Holmes, and you're my Watson."

There were a few others in the common room, and so I lingered to talk, and I found myself casting frequent glances out the window. It was black as pitch, and the north wind sent the trees and topiary to dance. I didn't see it at first, but there, under a streetlamp, stood the silhouette of a person. The sound of the twig snapping still echoed in my ears.

I excused myself from the conversation I was having with Jaunty and stepped out. Perhaps I am not the type to survive a horror movie, but I charged out the door and into the night. The figure stepped back into the darkness and was gone by the time I got to the lamp. I stood there in the darkness staring off into the shadows and trees for a long moment, and then I bolted back into the dorm, ran up the stairs and charged into my room, startling Colin, who was at his desk.

Nicholas lay under his blankets on his bed. I turned to Colin, "How long has he been there?"

Colin looked up at me, "An hour or so? Everything is quite all right, Hamster?"

I nodded as I plopped into my own bed, "Everything's peachy.

Chapter Twenty-Five

I always find a new bed turns up queer dreams, not necessarily bad but odd. That night, I dreamed of a tree that was a mountain, and then a hewn stump that was an island.

I awoke to the pale light of dawn, and feeling restless, I got out of bed and dressed for the day. Colin and Nicholas were still asleep. Colin lay with his hair sticking up in all directions, looking like a poorly groomed rooster. Nicholas had an odd, almost deathlike stillness in sleep – he slept flat on his back, his pale form barely stirring with each breath.

The others were no doubt taking advantage of the practice-free morning to sleep in. But I was already awake and eager to get away from the room, and from Nicholas. I grabbed my things, got dressed and walked down and into the sweet cold of morning.

A fire crackled in the hearth. Miss Dottie had slipped a few orange peels into the fire, turning the library into an orangery in spring. I opened my laptop, and after a moment I typed in, 'Dahlia Rook death'. And to my surprise, within seconds, several search results turned up, ranging from newspaper articles to YouTube videos to an entire community of amateur detectives on Reddit, each of whom had theories ranging from the disturbing to the ridiculous. U/Cryptidchaser, who was apparently hiking in the area, saw strange lights in the woods and so believed aliens to be involved! And so, as you can imagine, I decided to take my search elsewhere.

I am far better at listening than I am at reading, so I found a YouTube video from a channel called 'Buzzed and Unsolved' where two rather charming American gentlemen drink themselves silly by a campfire and discuss various unsolved crimes. I listened as they recounted various facts about my aunt's disappearance.

She was last seen at the manor walking towards the woods. After her disappearance, there was no ransom note or any such thing, so that meant it was not a kidnapping, nor was there money missing from her bank account, which made it unlikely she ran away. I closed my laptop.

It was rather odd that the articles were on her disappearance and not her death. Granny had told me that Dahlia had fallen from her horse; according to these articles, she was never found. My mind reeled, and I wondered how to raise it with Granny when I got back.

It was also quite strange reading all those theories and articles about my family. Her disappearance had been quite a big deal back then, as my family was rather renowned. My grandfather and grandmother were portrayed once on that ridiculous show 'The Crown'.

I looked out the library window to the looming cliffs and spitting sea. I found myself almost hypnotised by the dance of sea and stone. I tore my gaze away, looking around the library.

I took out the invitation card I'd found, and I stared at that face. A man's face woven from roots and boughs and leaves grinned up at me. At a glance, it was just a face – crudely etched, almost primitive. Something about the smirk was almost knowingly mischievous, like he knew some ancient dark secret the rest of us weren't privy to.

"Lord and Lady Greenwood…" I read again. And then, I walked over to the history section. I scanned the 'D' shelf and pulled out a copy of Debrett's peerage. I scanned it, flipping through the various Gs – Grangerfield, Greystone, Greydeer… but no Greenwood. I slid the book into its place, gathered my things and left for the dining hall.

Interesting… a crest and a title, but no peerage. The title did not exist, nor did it ever. Nor for the life of me could I find any coat of arms with that odd grinning face.

I was quite confused… whoever sent me those flowers (I wasn't so sure that it was Nicholas) and whoever sent Dahlia that invitation quite proudly called themselves Lord and Lady Greenwood. Why would these people lay claim to an utterly non-existent title?

Before I could consider much further, "Must say I am surprised to find you here, Hamsta!" a voice came, and I started. I was rather jumpy…you know… worrying about someone wanting to murder me.

"Oh, hello, Keyne," I said. Jago Keyne stood there smirking as always. I have never met someone so profoundly irritating. He dropped into the chair across from me, "Never took you for the studious type, Hamsta."

"Oh well, you will find I am full of surprises."

"You broke my heart, you know, Hamsta," he said, looking at me with a pouty sort of look.

"Oh, is that so?"

"You ditched me for our date… You were supposed to meet me in the clearing, remember?" he said in a chastising sort of voice.

"Well, other things were on my mind that day." I said, "If you recall, a gargoyle almost crushed my head in."

Jago gave a long-suffering sigh, "I do suppose I can forgive you just this once. But I utterly insist we reschedule for tonight."

Keyne really is very irritating. But, to his credit, he really did have a lovely smile, and his eyes were the precise colour of the Cornish sea at storm. And I remembered being utterly infatuated with him when I was younger; he had been the cool older boy with the cool hair, and I had hung onto his every word. But I only agreed because I figured he'd never ever shut up, "Okay, see you then."

He smirked yet again and pinched my cheek, "See you then, Hamsta."

I couldn't help the flush to my cheeks, but I rolled my eyes and outside the campus was awakening.

At brekkie, Regina informed me that Electra wanted to talk to the pair of us. So, at noon, we made our way over to the stables. Electra was brushing her horse and nodded a greeting when we walked in. "Might I ask you both a question?" Electra asked without truly asking, and her hand went brush, brush, brush.

Regina smiled graciously, "Of course. Do go on, darling." Electra cleared her throat, "Regina, why did you lie about being with my brother that night?

Regina seemed unfazed, "I did not lie. I assure you that your brother and I spent a good while in deep conversation. And the following morning, we were a couple."

Electra raised an eyebrow, "Oh, really? And pray tell, whatever did you talk about?"

Regina smiled, "I am a lady, Electra, my love. I don't kiss and tell."

Electra nodded, "Oh, but of course. Anyway, you should know my father thinks he did it," Electra said coolly, gaze held true. "Well, after the accident, my father called both of us into a room and demanded to know what Nicholas had done. Nicholas swore he was alone, and now I suppose he was just protecting... a lady's reputation. But the fact remains that the woman ended up dead on the snow that night."

"Lady Rook said she tried to leave and perhaps lost her way?" Regina said, and Electra shook her head, "No.... she had run herself a bath. Why would she do all that and then try to leave from the window? Someone tried to kill her."

Regina shot me a look, the sort that means 'play along,' and so I did. "Now hang on, Electra. Your brother was fond of that woman. You said so yourself. Why would he hurt her?"

Electra nodded, "Yes. As I said, he misses our mother, and that woman had sort of filled her place in our lives. I was quite fond of her, really, and I thought so was Nicky. But I think he had some sort of feelings towards her and lashed out like he always does."

"Well, I admit Nicholas does have violent impulses," Regina had said, but Electra interrupted.

"That's putting it mildly. The boy was violent from the first. Did you know he killed his cat with his bare hands? And you know how strange he has always been. Always getting into fights and all that," Electra said, the morning light playing over her pale features as she stared up at her horse, her hands brushing away.

Regina raised a delicate eyebrow, "his cat?"

Electra nodded, "Yes... Mother brought it for him, had it declawed and everything to make it safe for her little boy. He named it Midnight. Bloody thing followed him everywhere. One morning, I woke up, and it was dead, strangled. He was inconsolable and claimed to have not known what happened, but... but that is who he is."

I was rather horrified by this, but Regina furrowed an eyebrow, "So he killed a cat when he was a child, and now you think he killed a grown woman?"

Electra faltered, "Well, no… I just," she turned to me rather plaintively. "You know, Regina, in all those true crime stories… serial killers tend to start out by killing animals."

Regina's green eyes bore into her skull for a moment, "Well, I do suppose that is true."

"So, you and your father believe Nicholas to be guilty?" Regina asked.

Electra nodded, "Well… Dad does and well... I must confess, I do not love my father or Nicholas… obviously. But I love the Barking name. Nicholas is a danger to it and to himself. But if I manage to find proof of Nicholas' guilt, I might be able to save the name before Nicholas utterly smashes it."

"So," Regina mused, and there was something in her eyes, "What would you do with this proof? Blackmail your brother? Turn him over to a noose?"

Electra raised an eyebrow, "Well. Regina, you know how hard it is for a woman in our world. Take you or me. We're the oldest of our siblings, but we still don't inherit. Colin and Nicholas won't inherit because of any great competence on their part. They inherit for an accident of birth and the shape of their genitals. They get the money, the title, the power. They get the world. But if we want even a fraction of it, we must get into the mud and fight dirty."

Regina's smile was grim, and she said nothing. "Anyway," Electra said, "if you two were able to obtain proof he did it… You shall have my gratitude"

Regina sighed, "Well, I suppose if nothing else, you do know your audience, Electra, if anyone would be only too glad to get rid of Nicholas, it would be Hammy."

I rolled my eyes, but Electra only smiled, "Precisely, but your personal vendettas are the least of it. You know what my father is. When I take over when my time comes, you will need someone in that position to owe you a favour."

Regina smiled and studied Electra for a long moment. "I do suppose you have a point there… but do tell what it is you expect us to do?"

Electra dropped her brush into the pail and leaned against the stable door, "Well... you two and Nicholas are embroiled in some foul conspiracy… I know that, and you know that. There is no doubt in my mind you know the full truth of what happened that dark winter night…. but my father is wilfully blind and try as I might, I cannot convince him to see it."

I spoke for the first time, "Well… again, what do you want us to do?"

Her eyes seemed almost to shine in the morning light. "Well, it's quite simple. Nicholas has no love for either of you, nor you for him. But this shared… secret of yours means you all have to trust each other… work on that trust… exploit it and find me some real tangible proof of what he did. As I said, you will have my gratitude."

Regina was staring at Electra with the air of a child who has flipped over a rock and is poking at the slimy thing she found underneath. She lifted a hand and shook Electra's. "You know," she said, "I decided I like you, Electra Barking."

I nodded at her, "We will try our best." And we left Electra to her horses. When we were at a sufficient distance, Regina sighed, "All the Barkings are truly barking mad."

"I am inclined to agree," I said as we walked our breaths misting in the air, "that's the lovely thing about the Barkings, isn't it? Leave them alone, and they'll tear each other apart."

We walked in silence for a moment before I spoke, "How did Nicholas get into the room?"

She frowned, not breaking her stride, "What do you mean?" I shrugged, "Well, just that, Miss Smith's room was locked from the inside. How did Nicholas get inside to kill her?"

She froze in place, her smirk falling. She faltered for a moment, "Well… well, I don't know, but he obviously managed it. Perhaps he killed her, climbed down the trellis and attacked you?"

I scoffed, "Poor bastard can barely do a pull-up. I highly doubt he can make his way down an ice-cold trellis in the snow."

She shrugged, "Well, he confessed, and that's what matters, but perhaps we'd best do some research into our friend Miss Sarah Smith."

Chapter Twenty-Six

In the evening, the wind seemed to blow with a vengeance; it howled around the campus, rustling the leaves, creaking the branches and making the buildings rattle and shiver. I, being wise, was already safe and warm inside the towers, but outside, some hapless fools walked with hoods pulled low over their faces as they struggled against the gale.

I was quite tired, and so after a nice, long lukewarm bath, I crawled under my covers and wished Colin goodnight before giving myself over to sleep.

It was rather hard to sleep with the wind rapping at the window, it was maddening and chased me into my dreams.

Rap, rap, rap

In my dreams, I went back to Rook Moor, and I walked alone in a sea of dancing greys and greens. Jack's Tor loomed ahead larger and more imposing than in waking life. Men and women danced around it as a bonfire burned, spicing the sweet summer air with ash and woodsmoke.

Rap, rap, rap

The figures wore crowns of flowers and clothes of white; they danced and sang, and their laughter rose into the evening sky. Their faces were all at once familiar and strange, and I walked among them, but not with them. For nothing I could do could make them so much as look at me, much less break their rhythm.

But one of them was looking – a willowy girl with a sly smile and skin as brown as mine. She stood in the centre of the dancers, wearing a crown of golden flowers in her black hair. She winked at me and turned away.

I followed after her, following some strange dreamers' call, but I lost her to the crowd. And as I walked, all the others seemed to fall away like a retreating tide, and I was alone with the tor looming above me.

Rap, rap, rap

And suddenly I was awake, lying in bed, tangled in covers, and in the darkness, I could see Colin and Nicholas sitting awake, groaning and mumbling in annoyed confusion.

Rap, rap, rap

I realised then there was someone at the door. Colin hopped out of bed, grumbling and scruffy. There stood one of the older boys, Trombone Tromby-Smyth. He held a finger to his lips and then gestured for us to come out. Wordlessly, I grabbed my coat, swung it on and followed. Colin followed with his hair stuck up all about, and Nicholas followed in surly silence.

Archie had apparently been preparing because he'd come out in a coat and winter pants. Duffy mumbled, "Not this rubbish again," which earned him a sharp look from Trombone and caused him to duck behind Archie.

We followed Trombone onto the green where the girls were waiting, shepherded by Princess Georgina. Regina was mumbling about her beauty sleep, which earned her a slap from Georgina, which everyone knew was a bad idea because there was pin-drop silence, which broke when Regina turned around and slapped Georgina so hard that the princess went sprawling to the ground.

There was a loud 'Oooooh'. But Georgina was significantly less amused when she rose, spitting and shaking to her feet. "You best remember your place, De Winter," she said in a voice of forced cool. You De Winters ought to mind your betters."

Regina cocked an eyebrow, "Darling, you imagine yourself my better? We De Winters actually do something worthwhile. Your family is a bunch of little puppets we string up to entertain the plebs with your balcony waving and ribbon cutting… oh, and you got some spittle on your chin, dear." Regina said, wiping her kerchief at Georgina's face at some spittle loosed in her fury.

Georgina had drawn back her hand, but Trombone gripped her wrist. "We're already late, Georgie. Settle your scores later."

She huffed and puffed and ripped her arm free, but stalked away down the path.

We all followed in silence, although a few people clapped Regina on the back.

It was quite dark as we walked. A hare dashed down the path in front of me, and I stopped to watch as it paused briefly to stare at me before dashing into the tree line.

The stadium lights were off, and so the sports fields were dark and deserted. There was the odd cricket or hockey ball accidentally abandoned, and the guys and I made sport of kicking them back onto the field.

We went into the arts building, down a narrow wooden staircase, through a narrow wooden door. And into a large empty space that must have been a cellar or something like that.

In the centre stood Jago Keyne with his customary grin, "Ah, there you are, boys and girls. If you could all take a seat."

The air there was thick and heavy with old dust, but we all shuffled around, finding spots to sit on the cold, hard floor. Regina mumbled in my ear as she sat first, spreading her kerchief on the floor, "This place is overrun with dust. I'd rather not have my evening wear suffer the indignity."

Jago then stood in the centre, "Well, chaps and chapettes. Welcome to The Brotherhood of St Barts." He looked around as though expecting applause, but only got a bunch of tired and confused looks. Feeling bad for him, I clapped a little.

He smirked and rolled his eyes, "It would do you all well to express more excitement. The brotherhood is as old as this rock we live on, if not older."

Karan spoke up, "If that's so, then why haven't either of my parents mentioned it before? They talk about their time here a lot. Why would they not mention... this club of yours?" And there were echoes and sounds of agreement.

Jago's tone grew a trifle sharp, "First of all, Singh, it's not a 'club', it's an institution. And to answer your question. The brotherhood is sacrosanct. Members are forbidden from mentioning it to any but another member, and they hold to those vows to their deathbed."

Ignoring further questions, he turned to Trombone, Theo, and Georgina. "I think it's time we inculcate these little whelps in the pillars of the brotherhood."

They nodded, and he went on, "The first important principle is the principle of secrecy. Everything that we do here, everything we discuss, stays between us. Do you all understand?"

There were nods and sounds of agreement, and Jago nodded, "Good. Remember, though we might fight and scrape and scheme, we are a family. Our loyalty is the brotherhood first, our countries second. Understand?"

There were some exchanged looks, but again a sound of agreement. Jago nodded, "Good and now onto the next."

Theo stepped forward, holding a small bundle of sticks. There was a moment of silence while we watched him fumble with them.

Finally, he picked one up as we watched. "What happens when you break one stick?"

There was a pause as we realised it wasn't a rhetorical question and that he wanted an answer. Fiona spoke up. "It breaks, obviously."

"Exactly," Theo said, snapping the stick in half, tossing the pieces aside. "But what happens when you break two sticks?"

He said, picking up two of the sticks and holding them together. "You get four sticks?" said Colin slowly, looking confused, "Are you trying to test our arithmetic? We already did this in year two."

Theo rolled his eyes. "You're not seeing the point. What happens when you tie the sticks together?"

Duffy spoke up, looking utterly lost. "You get… a bundle of sticks?"

Theo sighed and looked to the heavens and muttered, what I assume was a prayer for patience. "Yes, a bundle of sticks…" he said, gesturing with the sticks and waiting for an answer.

Archie spoke, "Oh… the sticks that are together are much harder to break, right?"

Theo shot him a look. "Thank you, Aston, for that insightful analysis. Yes. The point is, we're stronger together than apart. Loyalty isn't just something you say; it's something you live and breathe. The brotherhood is your family. No matter what, you put each other first. Is that understood?"

Next, Georgina stood up, still bearing the mark of Regina's delicate hand on her cheek. She looked at us through her heavy, hooded eyes, "The next principle is obedience."

Regina spoke up before she could continue, "Terribly sorry to interrupt, darling Georgina, but isn't it a bit sexist to call it the brotherhood? Women are here too. Surely brotherhood is a bit outdated."

I am not sure if that was a genuine question or just Regina trying to needle Georgina, but the princess took it as the latter. She appeared to be struggling to keep her cool.

I chimed in, "Surely… siblinghood would be more appropriate." Next to me, Regina snorted, ducking her face to hide her amusement.

Georgina bit her lip before speaking, "Well, yes, of course, women are part of the institution and have been since the founding. And besides, Rook, siblinghood of St Barts doesn't really roll off the tongue the same way, does it?"

Jago cut in, "Anyway, tonight we're accepting you as honorary members. You're not really part of the brotherhood yet… you're just…guests."

"Precisely," Georgina spoke crisply. "Obedience is key to a well-functioning team. You need to be able to follow commands without question, even if they're dangerous or uncomfortable."

Her gaze flicked to Regina, who was still smirking defiantly.

"We all have our roles and duties within the Brotherhood," Theo continued. "Each position is essential to the group as a whole. We may be individuals, but we're collectively one entity. One unit… like a sports team.

Several heads bobbed in agreement.

"The next principle is trust," Trombone declared. "Can anyone tell me why trust is important?"

Harriet Caldwell-Wren spoke, "Trust is important to any institution, especially a family."

"Exactly," Theo said, looking at her with newfound respect. "Without trust, you have nothing. A chain is only as strong as its weakest link. We need to be able to depend on each other, implicitly."

There was some silence before Percival spoke up, "Well… are we part of it now?"

Jago scoffed, "As I said, in time… now I suggest you all run along back to bed. Oh, sleep lightly next Saturday. We expect you back here and with more energy and gratitude."

As we were led back out, the walls of the basement caught my eye; they had been carved with pocketknives and the like, mostly people writing their initials or diagramming love triangles.

Regina sauntered up to me; her hair was loose and tumbled over her pale shoulders. She was in a nightgown, but she wore it like an elegant evening dress.

"Darling," she said in her customary purr, "Are we having fun?"

"Oh, I am," I said, "It's rather adorably gothic. Do you think we might get to see a sacrifice?"

She laughed, "Oh, I do hope so. It might get terribly dull otherwise." Her laughing eyes were tracing the scratched and carved walls, "Besides… "

And she stopped short, grabbing my shoulder. "Hamlet, look at that," she said, jabbing at a section of the wall.

I stopped walking to look, causing a few people to bump into me and grumble off. It took a moment to see through the cacophony of carving, but deep into the rock was carved the words, "Lord and Lady Greenwood." We stood in silence for a moment. And below it was that crest crudely carved. The same grinning man and his regalia of flowers and vines.

"Who on earth are they?" I wondered, and perhaps too loudly, because several people broke from conversations and turned to look at us.

Jago sauntered over, "What's ever matter here?

Regina smiled sweetly, "Nothing at all, Jago. We were just adoring the…décor."

"Beautiful, isn't it?" Jago pouted at me, "But you two best be off, eh?"

Chapter Twenty-Seven

We returned to the Twins bone weary, and as I slid under my sheets, my feet hit something cold, hard and feathery. Confused, I lifted my sheets and felt a sickening lurch in my throat as I saw something black and bloody lying there. It took me a moment before I realised it was a dead bird, or more particularly a dead raven. Its neck was slightly cocked to the side, and its jet-black eyes were taking on a slightly paler tint.

"Hamlet," came Colin's voice. "Is that a bloody bird?"

All I managed to say was, "Well, it was."

A few of the other boys were coming in and out of their rooms, and they were all asking questions. Archie and Colin had wanted to call for a teacher. Scholar had come to see what all the fuss was about and was rather disturbed by the whole thing and shooed everyone back. He asked me to step aside into his room, but first to wrap the poor thing in old newspaper and remove it from public view.

"Hamlet," he said, sitting in his chair, "Is someone bothering you?"

I wasn't entirely sure how to answer, and so I merely shook my head. "Well, it's a raven."

He sighed deeply, pinching his nose, "Raven… rook most people won't differentiate, would they?"

"I know… I know," I said, staring at the sad bundle in my hands.

"So, I'll ask again," he said, "Are you having problems with someone? Barking, maybe?"

Barking. It had to be him, I thought. A message to be silent about the party or end up like the bird. I shook my head mutely, "It's just a prank."

He sighed, "Okay. I have to report this, you know?"

I nodded, and he sighed, "Will you get rid of that, please? I can't have my residents getting bird flu."

I obeyed, carrying it outside the dorm, and then I texted Regina, and soon she came down holding a tweed-coloured umbrella. Regina stared at the bird.

"I think, darling, someone means to silence you," she said, "You know I am always one to advocate that arguments between schoolmates should be solved between them, but as this is very clearly a threat of death, perhaps you should involve the headmaster."

I frowned, "I am not going to talk to Sir Hugh about it. I am sure we can figure it out without him."

She sighed and smoothed her hair, "Hamlet, you know Sir Hugh can be trusted. My mum and dad trust him implicitly. I am sure you are very upset about your detentions, but just swallow your pride, will you?"

I sighed, "Fine. What do we do with the bird?"

We ended up burying it under the leaves. I had half a mind to actually bury the poor thing, but I figured leaving it out in the open for its fellow birds and beasts to feast on allowed it to remain in the natural cycle after its life had been so unnaturally snapped short.

Then I went back to my dorm, and Colin helped me change my sheets while Nicholas watched silently and stone-faced. It had to have been him, or so I thought. But how?

Sunday morning came too fast, much too fast. We all had Mass in the great chapel.

And after that, we were free to do as we pleased with the rest of the day. But as there was much homework to be done, the darlings all congregated in our spot in the library. But not a lot of homework ended up getting done; Fiona was making one of those origami fortune tellers, Duffy was doodling, Archie was watching some of the recordings of our practices and had several pages of notes for all of us. Colin was leaning back in his chair, smiling in his sleep as the sunlit played over his features and turned his hair to fire.

I tried to do my homework, but there were too many thoughts in my head, and I needed to get them out.

Classes came and went that Monday in a dreary litany, and before long, I found myself in Old Hugh's dusty office. The tea that day was Earl Grey with a hint of ginger.

We were reading *Macbeth*, and by fate's funny hand, we ended up on the subjects of rooks anyway. We were reading Act II when we came upon the line that goes, 'Light thickens, and the crow/makes wings to the rooky wood.'

Sir Hugh said, setting down his aged copy, "Now, gentlemen, let us take a moment to appreciate the Bard's uses of words and imagery; thicken is certainly an odd word. A liquid thickens, a fog thickens, but does light?"

Nicholas's hand was the first in the air as always, not that he needed to rush. I never really bothered to answer Sir Hugh's stupid questions anyway. "He is describing dusk, Sir, by thickening, he can be taken to mean that the atmosphere grows denser and darker with approaching twilight, metaphorically representing Macbeth's many crimes and the deepening darkness of his psyche. Sir, and perhaps the line about the rooky wood… Well, Sir, crows and rooks are birds associated with death," he said this with a sideways glance at me, "So one can assume this foreshadows Macbeth's impending death at the forest of Birnam Wood."

Nicholas loves nothing but the sound of his own voice, and it took a great deal to ignore the slight. Sir Hugh then turned to me, "Well, Hamlet. What do you think?"

Shakespeare mentioned crows, too. That was odd, and it made me think about corvids, and so I suggested, "Well, rooks are gregarious; they live together in rookeries. But crows... are more solitary. But they are quite intelligent and are capable of solving puzzles."

Sir Hugh nodded, smiling broadly, "Precisely, Macbeth, through madness and murder, has isolated himself from the other lords and ladies. They turned against him, even backing the English invasion to unseat him. His isolation would be his downfall. Top notch, Hamlet."

I smiled, feeling pleased with myself. Nicholas nodded and smiled at me, which took me a little by surprise. I almost smiled back, but then I remembered the little gift he'd given me last night. Was the smile a taunt? For a moment, it seemed almost genuine.

"The point," Sir Hugh said, "Is that word choice is everything."

When the bell rang, Nicholas gathered his stuff and left. Sir Hugh seemed surprised that I was still there. "You're normally the first out the door, Hamlet. I assume you have either lost use of your legs or you have something to talk to me about."

I merely shook my head and slunk out. Something he'd said, 'word choice is everything,' had stuck with me.

I returned to my dorm room after dinner. I still had to read the rest of *Macbeth* for Drinkwater, and it really was utterly unreadable. I had read the same line thrice to little avail, and I tried again this time, reading it aloud to Colin:

"In the cauldron boil and bake; / Eye of newt and toe of frog Scale of dragon, tooth of wolf / Witches' mummy, maw and gulf / Of the ravined salt-sea shark, / Root of hemlock digged i'th' dark."

Colin snorted, "Sounds like a lovely casserole. We should try it sometime."

"Probably not the best idea," I said, "Hemlock's deadly poisonous, you know."

He'd said something in response, but I hadn't heard, for a realisation had hit me with the force of a blow to the head. "It was me… the white flowers." The window was open just a crack, letting in the sharp, salty air from the sea. Out over the water, the faint wailing of the Inchcape bell reached my ears. It was distant but distinct, like a whisper of some ancient warning. And, with a sudden flash, it reminded me of funeral bells tolling. My stomach twisted, though I couldn't say why.

"Colin," I said abruptly, leaning back in my chair. He looked up at me, his pencil still poised over his notebook. "Do you have a Bible?"

He nodded, "Yeah, on my desk." I crossed over and picked it up.

"'Beloved, never avenge yourselves, but leave room for the wrath of God, for it is written, Vengeance is mine; I will repay,'" says the Lord. "Instead, 'if your enemies are hungry, feed them; if they are thirsty, give them something to drink; for by doing this you will heap burning coals on their heads.'"

I closed the Bible and let it rest in my lap as my mind churned. I remembered the threat he'd hissed at me months ago, the hand gripping my collar like a vice. "Listen, Rook," he'd said, "you will not breathe a word of this to anyone." I remembered the sly smile he'd worn at five years old when his mother defended him after he'd picked a fight with me. And I remembered the rumours Electra had let slip about Nicholas and that cat – cruel whispers that hinted at something far darker than mischief.

"Don't tell me you've found religion, Hamster," Colin said, breaking into my thoughts.

I glanced up at him, half-smiling despite myself. "No, Colin. Just realising that word choice is everything.

Hemlock. He'd poisoned her with hemlock.

Chapter Twenty-Eight

For now, the days passed as they always did – classes, practice, and evenings spent in the library or the dorms. Nicholas was quiet, keeping to himself, though every so often I'd catch glimpses of him in odd, solitary moments.

I looked for any sign that gave away his guilt, any taunt, however subtle, but none came. The Nicholas I'd known never passed up a chance to cast me a sneer or a sly verbal jab. I'd expected it, even grown accustomed to it. But somewhere, since those cold January days, I realised that the Nicholas I had known had been dying since that summer day his mother died.

I found the anger and hatred of years slowly ebbing away, and I wasn't sure what it was I felt – pity… guilt… regret? Some noxious mixture of all the above. At times when I saw him sitting alone during dinner or curled up away from the world in his bed, I almost reached out, but drew back, afraid he'd snap at me and chase me off.

And the darndest thing, I wasn't entirely sure anymore that he had killed that woman. But he had confessed to Regina, "It was me… it was me… the white flowers."

And then there was that Bible verse of his: if your enemies are hungry, feed them; if they are thirsty, give them something to drink."

I had already told Regina about the hemlock, and together, we had arranged a meeting with Electra at the stables. I had told her everything – the speech, the flowers, the Bible verses. But even as I was speaking, something gnawed at the edges of my mind. A memory, half-formed, buried beneath the weight of all that had happened that weekend.

Electra had scoffed. "Hemlock," she echoed. "Seems the little bastard's style, I suppose."

Regina lifted her chin, smiling as though we had simply bested a rival in a game of chess. "I suppose now, Electra darling, you owe us one."

Electra's lips curled into a slow, deliberate smile. "But of course."

And yet—

"Hang on," I interrupted, the doubt digging deeper until I was unable to stop myself. "He poisoned her with hemlock… but then how did she fall out of the window? And how did her body move? And who attacks—"

Electra sighed, rubbing her temple. "Rook, don't be tedious. Hemlock causes respiratory failure… akin to choking. She must have opened the window for air, panicked, and fallen out. In her confusion, she must have been the one who attacked you."

Regina nodded, as if this were the most natural thing in the world. "That tracks."

The explanation was neat. Too neat. The kind of explanation that should have made perfect sense, and yet—

I frowned. "Does it? If she were already poisoned, already dying, wouldn't she have been too weak to fight? Too weak to move, even?"

Electra rolled her eyes. "People in mortal distress do all sorts of inexplicable things. Survival instinct, final bursts of energy. The power of a mind dying can surprise you."

She waved a hand dismissively. "She panicked. She lashed out. And ran off. Mystery solved."

I shook my head. "I don't know… I just… something doesn't feel right."

Electra exhaled sharply, suddenly looking at me as though I were particulariy slow. "Oh, for God's sake, Hamlet. If you want to feel guilty for getting Nicholas Barking his just desserts, then wallow in it. But don't waste my time with pointless doubts."

I couldn't quite chase away the unease gnawing at the edges of my mind.

Regina's hand clamped around my arm. "No buts, darling. We should be going."

I let her lead me away, my thoughts still tangled, something still wrong.

"What has gotten into you?" she murmured as we walked, her voice warm with amusement, but edged with something sharper. "You solved the case, darling. You should be *proud.*"

"That's the thing," I said. "I'm not so sure I did."

Had I just condemned an innocent man? As innocent as Nicholas Barking could ever be, that is.

When we got back, it was late, and the campus was cloaked in the kind of deep, undisturbed silence that settles over everything on winter nights. I sat at my desk, under the yellow glow of a single lamp, trying for the umpteenth time to jot down my thoughts about the past few weeks. The paper was covered in scribbles and crossed-out lines, each sentence more futile than the last. I'd never been much for writing, but something about this – about him – compelled me to try.

Nicholas sat at his own desk. And I found myself studying him – the black hair, the pale skin and the blue eyes. And I found myself studying his desk too. I'd never really notice it before, preferring to ignore his section of the room entirely, but that day, something on it caught my eye.

A framed picture of a boy and a cat. I rose to my feet and strolled over to peer at it from over his shoulder. It was little Nicholas with a scruffy black kitten on his lap. In that picture, I only saw a little boy of a frail build with blue eyes, gently holding his pet. I found myself wondering… was that Nicholas as his mother saw him?

He caught me looking and looked up, "Can I help you, Rook?"

"Sorry," I said, "Is that your cat?" I asked, aware I was sounding very stupid.

He looked confused, and I didn't blame him, as that was probably the longest conversation we ever had without it escalating to blows. "Yes, Midnight," he said finally, "Had him as a boy."

I didn't quite know what to say. I'd remembered, of course, the dark tale Electra told me about the cat, but I found myself hard-pressed to believe it somehow.

Nicholas half turned back to the picture. "He was my only friend," he said at last, "When I was young… I never got along with the others. I preferred books to people. My mum tried to socialise me," he said with a chuckle, "invited people around and threw parties, but it never really stuck. She got me the kitten when I was seven… It's a bit like a piece of you dies when they die, isn't it?"

He turned back to his computer and ended the conversation, and as I stared at the little boy and his kitten safe beneath the glass pane, I felt a flickering of doubt return.

I went back to my own desk, and I found myself thinking of Baskerville.

Chapter Twenty-Nine

That Friday was an odd silver grey. The sun hadn't seen fit to grace us, but the weather had marginally strayed from hellishly cold to almost bearably cold. I took the opportunity to go for a long ride. After classes, I went out to the stables, and it was just the horses and me. Dufffy's Marmalade neighed in greeting, and so I gave him a carrot and a pat on the nose.

Electra's horse stood silent as ever, watching me. A pale white mare with eyes as blue as those of its mistress. Her name was Cannibal, so called for her ill temper and habit of biting the other horses, and well, anyone other than Electra who approached her. And so, I kept a good distance from her as I made my way to Scoundrel. That's what I named him – quite appropriate, I thought!

He and I have long since come to an understanding and one of mutual respect. He and I are a lot alike, I suppose (other than both being brown). Both of us hate being told what to do.

I rode him out onto the beach with the spray of the sea in his hair as the wind whipped at us. One of the rare moments we got on really.

We rode fast and hard, but not so fast that I could escape my thoughts. They caught up with me: thoughts of Nicholas, and hemlock and Dahlia. Despite his confession, despite the seemingly overwhelming evidence against him… something was nagging my mind, but I couldn't put my finger on it.

Don't get me wrong, if Nicholas Barking had to kill someone, he would use poison. He is far too subtle (read cowardly) to use a knife, a bat or a gun. Believe me, I have no great faith in his gentle nature or whatever cliche… There was something else bothering me, but I couldn't for the life of me put my finger on what exactly.

I suppose the most obvious question is where on earth did he get it from? Not like it grows on the grounds. Mother's gardeners take care of that, especially with Baskerville around. It does grow out on the moors, but I don't see Nicholas Barking braving the cold to venture out on Rook moors.

I rode until the tallest of the campus towers was hidden by the trees, and I dismounted. I tied Scoundrel to a lone tree and sat on the damp sand. We were alone there, just us and the sea and the winter-blighted forest behind us. I found myself thinking of Lady Moira. She had been an intense woman. Always doing something; she was very involved in the PTA, or always volunteering for something or the other.

She was one of those people who seemed almost allergic to sitting down – a person who took life head-on, and never flinched away from anything. She was always quarrelling too, with teachers, other parents, waiters and whatnot. Despite her many faults, she was a strong woman, and she loved her children fiercely. I realised then that there was no way that woman would ever have taken her own life. Which meant only one thing… Moira Barking had been murdered.

But why? And by whom?

I stayed there until I felt the pain in my head, a dull, constant companion the past few days, faded away. Then I returned Scoundrel to the stables, fed him a glut of carrots and went back to campus.

I had half a mind to go to the library and join the others, but my phone buzzed. I had gotten an email from the campus mail centre that a parcel had arrived for me. So, I went off to fetch it.

It was a package from Mother; she'd sent some sweets and other stuff. And for which I was duly grateful.

Just then, Nicholas Barking strolled into the mail hall, picked up a letter and sauntered into a corner to open it. I pretended to be busy myself. I couldn't help but notice the envelope was pure black. And though Nicholas' face was inked with shadows, I could see the tension in the pale lines of his face. I could see the way his face drained of colour as his eyes scanned the letter within. His eyes danced up and down the paper several times as though unable or unwilling to believe what he was reading. I almost wanted to call out, ask what it was that was bothering him, but I knew it wouldn't be welcome. And so, all

I did was watch as Nicholas closed his eyes, took a deep shuddering breath as though trying to steady himself and crumpled the letter into his pocket.

I couldn't help myself and followed him from a distance. He walked rapidly beneath the tree-lined pathways past groups of people and back to the towers. The rain was falling by then, a cold sting that made the barren branches dance and turned the pavement to patent leather. Ignoring the prefect, he stormed into the common room searching around wildly till his eyes landed on Regina.

Regina stared in shock for a moment before getting up, "Oh, Nicky darling. Look at you, you'll catch your death like that," she said sweetly as she strolled over to him.

Nicholas did not respond; he didn't look at anyone. And he flinched away from Regina's ministrations. Then he seemed to steel himself, and his shaking quelled. He stood up straight. He shoved the letter into Regina's face, "It was you, wasn't it?"

The violence of the shove sent her back a few steps, but she steadied herself. Archie and Fiona had sprung to their feet, but she raised a hand to stop them. Her tone was as sweet as sugar and sharp as broken glass, "Whatever do you mean, Nicholas?"

He snarled, whirling around to face me and pointing at both of us, "*Both* of you!" he barked, "With your sneaky little letters."

Regina cast a bemused look at me, "Letters? What on earth are you talking about?"

He made a sound… that half laugh, half snarl, "Oh don't play the innocent, De Winter… you and Rook… you're the only ones who know. You think you're sly with your little subtle taunts?"

Regina and I exchanged a blank look. The room was pin-drop silent, and everyone was watching us. Nicholas stood up to his full height, "You think you can blackmail me? well… I'm done playing your little game."

He whirled on his heel and stormed out. "What was that about?" I muttered to Regina. For once, she had no answer.

Chapter Thirty

3rd February, 2024
Saturday

It was a rather rainy Saturday when Nicholas Barking confessed to murder. Regina and I had spent the evening pondering over the odd things he accused us of, and arrived at the conclusion he'd taken leave of his senses. Anyway, it was all for nought, for at about 11:40 at night, the door to the common room swung open and Nicholas stood in the doorway shivering, shaking and soaked to the bone.

Nonetheless, he strode over to Regina and me. "Well, I have already called my father and informed him," he said in a cool, calm, rather business-like tone, "You have no power over me anymore."

Regina cast a look at me and then turned back to Nicholas, "What on earth are you on about?"

Nicholas took another moment to steel himself and turned to the others, "It was me."

"What were you?" Colin asked, "Barking, are you running a fever?"

Regina reached out a hand to touch his forehead, but he slapped it away, "Sorry," he said, "I… I killed her. Je— Jen— Sarah Smith. I killed her."

Regina's face was ghostly white. Nicholas Barking's eyes locked on me, "It was the little white flowers, you see." He smiled faintly and whispered, "I suppose I must thank you for that… wouldn't have been able to do it without you."

The room went as quiet as a crypt, and the pitter-patter of raindrops was like an artillery bombardment. Nicholas nodded, "Well, my father shall be here soon. I should go pack. Thank you all." And with that, he turned and walked up the stairs to Bachelor's Tower.

It was odd, you know. It should have been a moment of triumph, but even then, it felt wrong. Regina looked up at me, "What on earth was that about? What's he on about flowers?"

I watched Nicholas retreat up the stairs, "I genuinely have no idea."

It was all the school could talk about, and as expected, a lot of the curiosity and intrusive questions were directed at Regina and me. But we ignored all of them, even Fiona, who stomped away promising never to talk to us again, only to ask us to watch *Pretty Little Liars* with her ten minutes later.

Then Electra had sent us a rather rude summons over text, so we went over and found her on the shooting range with two shiny old hunting rifles in her grip. She tossed one at Regina, who caught it effortlessly. "I do believe you, and I have a score to settle, De Winter."

Regina locked and loaded her rifle. "Why yes, we do."

Electra snapped her fingers at me, "Be a dear, will you, Rook? And operate the machine for us."

I nodded and went over to the machine and waited for them to give me the signal. Electra spoke up, "I'll go first, shall I?" She stepped up to the mark and took aim. I pulled the lever, and the little disk flew. Electra's finger squeezed the trigger, and it shattered, littering the grass with shards of ceramic.

"I heard my little brother confessed," she said, her voice deceptively cool, "Confessed to all and sundry, apparently. It's all over the campus, and people have been hounding me rather incessantly about it."

Regina and I exchanged a brief glance as she stepped up. I let the pigeon go, and she aimed, shot and met her mark. Electra went on, "And I heard he mentioned something about letters you two sent him? It appears he figured just spilling his dark secrets to the world was preferable to being blackmailed by you two. That is to be expected, of course, he would hate to have a leash on him. He's awfully predictable that way. I do admire his boldness, but that rather scuppers it all, doesn't it?" Regina exchanged another look with me while we waited for Electra to take her shot. The disk sliced through the air and shattered. "Electra," Regina began, "We have no idea what Nicholas was talking about. We wrote him no letters."

Electra raised an eyebrow, "Oh, is that so? Well, you'll have to forgive me if I don't believe you… seeing as the three of us were the only people on this island who knew the truth."

There was nothing I hated more than being accused of something I didn't do, and so I spoke up, "You must think the two of us are as stupid as your brother is. Believe or don't believe, Barking, but we didn't write him any letters."

Electra whirled, her face pale and drawn, but before she could respond, Regina cut in, "You Barkings are so delightfully entertaining. Ever willing to turn each other over. You in particular, Electra darling, you never passed up a chance to screw over your brother, did you? The only person who hates Nicholas more than Hamlet is you." I had a sudden flash of memory from Pre-K. Every day, Electra would accompany Lady Barking to pick up Nicholas, and when Moira wasn't looking. Electra would pinch him till he cried.

Electra opened her mouth to respond, but Regina cut across, "Yes, yes, I'm sure you're just quaking with impotent rage, but how about we talk about something constructive… hmm?" She locked, loaded and scored a perfect shot. "Hamlet has a rather fascinating theory, which I think you might like to hear."

Electra turned to me, and I swallowed, "I have been doing something thinking about that. Remember at the party, he smacked his father's wine glass from his hands?" I said, "He ran from the room."

"Do you mean," Electra said, her voice oddly excitable, "That he meant to target our father?"

I hadn't wanted to vocalise those words myself. Lord Barking… I adore the man, and the possibility of his being murdered by his son was too horrible to admit, and it made me loathe Nicholas all the more.

Regina turned to her, "What do you suppose will happen to him now?"

Electra shrugged, "Don't worry, you two… I'll deal with him." She tossed her rifle at Regina's feet, "Clean up, won't you, darling?" and she sauntered off.

Regina's green eyes glared at Electra retreating back. I stood next to her, "Poor dear was in quite a rage about that confession… and those letters."

Once again, it had all been for nothing. Lord Barking arrived that night, or so the story went. By the time I made it to the room, he had already packed and gone. His space was stripped bare, emptied with the cold efficiency of someone accustomed to sudden departures.

I'd heard through whispers, passed from one hushed voice to the next, that Nicholas had been retrieved by none other than an irate Lord Barking himself. The story went that the two of them climbed into Barking's sleek black Jaguar and vanished down the road. I wasn't sure how Lord Barking managed to get his car to the island until I heard there was a ferry, seldom used, reserved for discreet arrivals and departures to the nearest port.

Regardless, he was gone. And the strange part? I barely had to lift a finger. Yet the victory, if it could be called that, rang hollow. I stood in silence, staring at the crumpled piece of paper in my hand… the one I had so titled *'Proof Barking killed That Woman'* and tossed it into the fire, watching it curl, blacken and vanish in the flames.

"This just settles it," Fiona said as she peeled a banana at dinner, "Nicholas pushed the woman out of the window. The old Barker decided Nicholas was far too dangerous to roam around in public."

Duffy nodded enthusiastically, "Do you reckon he had something to do with Lady Barking's death as well?"

"It's certainly possible," Fiona said, "The poor lad has always been rather touched in the head. And quite volatile too… perhaps she didn't let him have a biscuit before dinner, and he decided to do her in."

Regina's eyes briefly met mine before returning to Fiona, "Don't you think, darling, that our Nicholas is far too much of a mother's boy to kill his own mother?"

"Oh, I am not saying it was pre-planned or something of the sort," Fiona said, "I am saying it happened in a moment of anger. A crime of passion, as they say."

Archie scoffed, "Hang on, I agree with Regina. Now, while Barking might have been a bit barking, I hardly believe he was the type to lash out against his mother. All his little tantrums were against us. He was always so sweet with the teachers and parents."

"Besides, if Nicholas were to kill anyone, it would probably be his father," Windsor interjected, "Old Harry was always so very strict and short with Nicholas. Oh, and get this, Harry was petitioning my grandfather and parliament to alter the Barking title so that it would be inherited by the eldest heir, rather than simply by the male heir."

Regina's head snapped around so fast that Polly flinched, "Windsor, do you mean to tell us that Lord Barking was trying to disinherit Nicholas in favour of Electra?"

Everyone at the table was staring at Windsor with their mouths agape. "Windsor, my old chum, why on earth did you not tell us this before?" Archie said.

He shrugged, "I hardly thought you lot would find petty court drama so fascinating."

Archie promptly cuffed him on the back of the head, "Don't be an idiot, Windsor," he said.

Regina frowned, "Windsor, from now on, I expect you to tell us any and all tidbits of 'petty court drama', especially where it concerns our apparently murderous friends."

He rubbed his head, "Oh, alright," he said, elbowing Archie in retaliation, "I apologise. It might interest you all to know that they have decided to redo the bathrooms at Buckingham. The tiling used to be black and white and will now be maroon and white."

Regina rolled her eyes. "Hang on," I said, "What for? I quite liked the black and white." Regina shot me a look of great annoyance, and I frowned, "Oh, come. It was like a big chessboard. Although I suppose there are maroon and white chessboards, right?" Well, I am rather fond of Buckingham Palace as I was a cupbearer to His Majesty when I was younger, back when my grandfather was still Prime Minister.

"Oh. Well, Windsor, are they sticking with the square-shaped tiles?" I asked. Regina rolled her eyes again, and I wondered why she wasn't feeling dizzy, "Anyway… Windsor, would you be so kind as to tell us more about Lord Barking's petition?"

Windsor nodded and gestured emphatically with his chicken drumstick, "Oh yes. Well, the Barking title is created so that the male heir would inherit even if he had an older sister. Many of the old titles were created like that."

I nodded, "Ours too. But my great-grandfather had it changed so that the eldest heir could inherit regardless of gender."

Windsor nodded, his mouth full of chicken, "Exactly, Lord Harry cited that as a precedent. And apparently, it caused quite the upset in the Barking household. Lady Barking, for once, was quite against it."

Regina was quiet for a moment, "So, Nicholas had another reason to despise his father."

Windsor nodded, "But to attaint one's own son and heir is no simple matter."

Regina met my gaze, and I knew what she was thinking… motive. If Nicholas had gotten wind of Lord Harry's petition, he would have had the motive to want to kill his father. But the odd thing was, why on earth would he do it so publicly? Surrounded by not only most lords and ladies, but CEOs, foreign world leaders and the Prince and Princess of Wales themselves?

Humiliation, I had supposed, but that would be beyond stupid. No way such a death wouldn't be investigated, and they would pursue his killer to the ends of the earth. Perhaps he realised that, and that was why he'd changed his mind at the last moment and knocked the glass from his father's hand. But somehow the glasses had gotten mixed up, and Sarah Smith got his father's glass.

Poor Sarah Smith. She wasn't even the intended victim.

"Anyway, darlings," Fiona had said, "Let's talk about something that isn't quite so loathsome as Nicholas Barking."

"Oh. There is this marvellous documentary about the Graveman," Polly said.

Archie shrugged, "Well, spoiler alert, they never catch the guy. Now you know the ending."

"Oh, Archie, don't be so dull," Polly said, "It's not about the ending; it's a terribly fascinating documentary, and it goes rather in-depth about this fellow. You know the bit about the flowers he'd strewn about the graves? They all apparently had their own meaning. In the Victorian secret language of the flowers."

Regina looked at me, and I held her gaze. "Do you know anything about this Victorian language, Polls?" I'd asked. "What do dahlias mean?" Regina and I were still looking at each other.

"Oh. Well, they hadn't been brought over yet, so the Victorians weren't even aware of them. But irises mean that one sends a message, white lilies represent one's love is pure, pansies say someone is thinking of you, and Queen Anne's lace means safety."

I was about to sip from my glass when I remembered something Nicholas had said about white flowers and then something about hemlock. I gasped so loudly that Colin stared.

"That Barking idiot," I said.

Chapter Thirty-One

Sunday night

"Library 9:00. Bring no one."

The little bottle of nail polish rattled a bit as she set it down. Regina fixed me with a gaze that was sharp as a knife's edge.

"Now, darling, I am about to tell you something rather shocking," and she leaned in, "But first… I need you to tell me why you think Nicholas is innocent. He confessed, and you were so dead sure of his guilt only a few days ago."

I sighed, looking at the skeletal tree branches waving outside the window, "Back in December, before the rest of you lot showed up. I was in my room, and Nicholas came in. I was quite irritable about something, and he was making what I thought was small talk, but he was looking over one of my terrariums, and he mentioned something about white flowers. And then the following day, I noticed one of my terrariums was disturbed and that plants were missing. Nicholas thought the flowers were hemlock… but they were Queen Anne's lace… quite harmless."

Regina was silent for a moment and then laughed, "Oh, that stupid boy."

"I quite agree," I said, "He is a very stupid boy, but now… It's your turn. Come on, then tell me."

She smiled and leaned back lethargically in her chair, blowing on her nails to dry them, "How do you think Moira Barking died? It wasn't in the papers, and the parents won't tell us, but darling, I think we both know."

I swallowed, remembering Old Hugh's words, "She took her own life, didn't she?"

"Oh well, so it would seem, don't interrupt me," she said crossly, "She was found in her bed quite dead. Apparently, they thought it was a heart attack, but they found a note of farewell in her bag, and when the coroner turned out the contents of her stomach, they found traces of poison. But Nicholas thinks she didn't do it to herself, and he also thinks it wasn't an accident."

"No", I said after a moment, "She was obsessed with her children, especially with Nicholas. She would never kill herself and leave them.

"Indeed," she said with a nod, "That's why Nicholas himself reasoned. That his mother would never willingly leave him and Electra."

"So it must have been some sort of a freak accident," I said, "Right?"

"No, Hamlet," Regina said, almost with a dramatic flourish in her voice, "She was murdered." Then, before I had any time to process it, she went on, "Guess who he thinks killed her?" Then, without giving me time to guess, "Your mother and his father… and here's the why. She found out about their affair."

"But that was obvious to all, wasn't it?"

"Perhaps, but not to Nicholas it would seem," she said, "Your mother is a single woman, and so, I suppose Lord Barking was having an affair with her. Ah, the power of words," she said quietly.

"Hamlet, Nicholas himself stumbled upon them one day in Lord Barking's office. They explained it away, but he knew what was going on. Oh, and apparently Nicky was seven, and so this affair has been on at least half our life spans."

I sat in silence for a moment, looking back on my whole life and a thousand small moments. Lord Barking, while not there all the time, was something of a consistent presence. Mother would always sit next to him. Lord Barking was the first person Mother called the day grandfather died. Then there were the rather frequent golf trips.

"It's been going all my life," I shrugged, "Well, even so, Lord Barking has been a bigger part of my life than my own father. And my mother, even though she is having an affair with a married man… I don't see her killing someone, and Lord Barking … being involved in his wife's death just doesn't make sense."

"And, you know how we talked about how he is the 'spin doctor', well, the man breathes and weaves narrative. If he had wanted his wife dead, he would have done it in a far less suspicious circumstance than poisoning her in their own bedroom," she said.

"And what about that woman? Sarah Smith?" I said, "Is she connected to Lady Barking's death?"

Regina smirked, "Yes… and no. Do you remember when I called the prep school in London?"

"No."

"Well, I did. To ask them if they have any record of such a teacher working with them. Well, they did not. And what's more is that Lord Barking or someone representing him via letter had apparently opted out of the school's offered homeschool teacher programmes. And preferred to simply have lesson plans sent to them."

"So… she wasn't a teacher?" I asked, flabbergasted, "Who was she?"

Regina shushed me, "Be patient, darling, I was just getting to that. Anyway, I did a search for the name Sarah Smith, and it turned up a few people, none of whom looked anything like our Miss Smith. And then I searched through obituaries for women who died on or near December 22nd, and found a singular report of a woman, Jenny Leach. Now, Miss Leach was a private investigator."

"*What*?"

"Pipe down, darling, else you'll wake up the whole school," Regina said coolly, "I put the few pictures I could find that had her in it through Second Eden's reverse search engine and well. Miss Leach was apparently involved in a lot of rather high-profile cases. Such as Frederick Usher's divorce, and other messier matters… but yes, our dear, lamented Sarah Smith was just a front. Her real name was Jenny Leach."

I was silent for a moment as I mulled that over, "When we left Cimmerian Manor back in autumn, Nicholas threatened us to keep quiet. I guess this is what he was talking about. He was so certain about his dad and my mum being behind Lady Moira's death that he hired someone to prove it…"

Regina rolled her eyes, "Got to love that trademark Barking genius. Anyway, someone else at that party must have realised she was an imposter. That would make her Lord Barking's imposter and make Nicholas, Lord Barking's traitor."

Images of a shadowy black figure stalking the tinsel halls with a knife crept through my mind. "Well… now what shall we do?"

Chapter Thirty-Two

Wednesday
7th February, 2024

Well, I had meant to stop writing once I got to that conversation, but I found keeping a diary or journal or whatever it was, rather therapeutic.

Well, anyway, Regina, she'd read the diary and had said rather contemptuously and yet somehow kindly, "Oh Hamlet, you poor thing, you are rather hypermetropic, aren't you?"

"What on earth is that supposed to mean?" I snapped. My wrist was throbbing from scribbling out multiple chapters for her amusement, and instead of being nice, she was… well, being Regina.

"Oh. just that you focus on what's right in front of you rather than what's really happening. Or you know the phrase 'miss the forest for the trees?' Well, that's pretty much you."

"Regina, if this delightful session of compliments could kindly wrap itself up and get to the point, I would greatly appreciate it," I said, doing my best to keep my voice calm despite the throbbing irritation building behind my eyes.

She gave me one of those exasperating smirks and said, "Well, despite your almost deeply concerningly obsessive levels of detail in writing this diary, you somehow managed to include a clue without even realising it yourself. That's impressive in its own way, I suppose." I resisted the overwhelming urge to yank her hair. Instead, I folded my arms and replied, "Actually, I already know who the killer is."

Her eyebrows shot up, and she looked at me as though I'd just announced that I'd discovered Atlantis. "You're insane," she declared flatly after hearing my hypothesis. Naturally, this led to an argument, which inevitably turned into a bet. Now, we're racing to gather proof to pin the crime on our respective suspects. God help us both. May the best man (me) win.

Also in other news, Sir Hugh had insisted on keeping up detentions even though Nicholas was no longer there. At detention the day following Nicholas' removal, I went to his office, and I dropped into my customary chair and took out my books and my pen.

He frowned, "I expected you to be happier. Is that not almost exactly what you wished for?" I dropped my gaze and didn't say anything.

Sir Hugh nodded, "More often than not, I find that when given a chance, hate gives way to empathy. It's harder to hate someone when you actually understand them, isn't it?"

"I wouldn't say I understand him fully yet," I looked out the window and on the sunlit green, some of the boys and girls were kicking a ball around, "One has to talk with someone to properly understand them. But, Sir, I know… about Lord Barking and my mother."

His face showed no shock. "I am not surprised. The pair of them has made little attempt to keep it a secret."

I laughed watching the sunlight turn dust motes into fireflies. He chuckled and under his bushy brows, his blue eyes crinkled, "And how do you feel about it?"

I looked up at him, "Is it awful that I am not outraged? They make each other happy. And I know it's a great sin to ruin a marriage, but you know…"

He smiled a little, "You and Nicholas are so alike, and yet so different. He has been quite upset about it. Ever since he'd found out, he was quite young and well… it seems to have shaken him deeply. Filled him with this great anger, and of course, his father and your mother were quite beyond the reach of his anger. But you weren't. I know it wasn't fair for him to blame you for something you had no say in… but it was a child's logic."

"I do find it just a bit hypocritical," I said, "Both him and his mother. I had no part in what Mother and Lord Barking did."

Sir Hugh smiled grimly, "Well, I am afraid that to be human is to be inconsistent."

"When we were around five or so, my dog, Baskerville, accidentally knocked Nicholas over. Poor Nicholas was rather shaken up. His mother was furious and demanded that Baskerville be put down. But Lord Barking laughed and told Nicholas to man up. I'm not going to say I feel softer towards Lady Barking, but now… I can't help but feel microscopically sorry for Nicholas." I glanced quickly at Sir Hugh, then looked away. Sir Hugh smiled. "You see, in that moment, he was just a scared child who turned to his father for solace and was spurned." He chuckled. "I suppose the curse that comes with having a perfect memory is that you remember all the slights made against you. But with Nicholas, the two of you never gave each other a chance for anything else. Yet certain truths seem to have brought you two together."

I sipped my Earl Grey. "Lord Barking has quite the temper," I whispered.

Sir Hugh nodded, "He does indeed. Certainly, he can be charming and even loving, and he does love his son. But Harry has certain expectations and is not pleased when they are not met."

I had decided that I quite liked Sir Hugh's office. The large windows allowed for ample natural light, and so he never really used his ceiling lights during the day. I found his room quite a relaxing place to be, really. But outside, the sun was shining, and I longed for a nice walk on the beach, away from the world. "Sir… since Nicholas is no longer here, will we be continuing with these detentions?"

He seemed almost bemused. "Nicholas no longer being with us does not pardon you. Besides," he said with a grin, "I rather enjoy the time we spend together."

I tried not to sigh. Sir Hugh chortled, "Oh. Cheer up, Lord Hamlet. If you wish, we need not discuss Shakespeare."

"What… what was he like when he was in the academy? What was Mother like? All of them, what were they like?" I asked, "You told me a little bit, but I want to hear more."

Sir Hugh closed the book in front of him, "It's interesting, really, having watched them grow up and change, and somehow not change at all at the same time. I was their teacher then. I became Headmaster later. They are all older. Some are a little happier, and some are a little sadder. But I find on the whole, they are all mostly the same as they were when they were children."

I sipped my tea, "How do you mean?"

He smiled sadly, "Harry, I find, has changed the least, though I imagine he thinks he has changed the most. He was, as I have told you, an accomplished athlete and student, but he also had a love for drama. He and your mother acted in a lot of Shakespearean plays. Their favourite was Hamlet."

"Harry, even back then, was very good. I wouldn't call him a liar exactly; he was very good at using facts… rather carefully selected to spin facts to suit his fiction," Sir Hugh said dryly, "I suppose he'd been training all his life for his position."

"Was he always so...?" I stuttered, looking rather desperately for a word

"Volatile?" Hugh provided. "Oh, yes and no," he went on, "he was always rather unforgiving when he thought something wasn't up to his standards. And he had a rather militaristic style of captaincy. But still he was quite charming, jovial and quick to laugh. He was a natural leader; people looked to him even then. There was the incident with his leg, and he lost out on a rather promising career in sports. His father, Charles, the twelfth Duke of London, was jubilant as it meant his son had to take over the business after all, and he did have such a natural talent for it."

"Mother and Rosie… what were they like?"

He leaned back a little in the chair, "Your mother and Rosemary were inseparable back then, as now. They and Harry formed a happy little threesome. They had quite a little group around them, but they were at its core in a way. Your mother was quite the same way now as she was then. Headstrong, determined and—"

"Bossy?" I suggested

Sir Hugh laughed, "Yes. I suppose you can say that. Of course, she is an incredibly bright woman, and they can come across as bossy. Although I must say if people listened to your mother more often..." And he tapered off into a chuckle.

"Sir?" I asked, taking advantage of the momentary silence, "What was my aunt like?"

Sir Hugh's face darkened, "Dahlia?" He echoed and was silent for a moment, "She was quite… quite a spirited young woman… always off with the fairies as they say." He went silent for a moment, watching the sun dip into the horizon, "You know… it is Friday, and it has been a terribly long week. Why don't we end early? Go and enjoy the sunshine, Lord Hamlet."

Chapter Thirty-Three

Friday
9th February

After classes and practice and whatnot, Regina and I went to the school tea room. Quite a quaint little place, elegantly furnished in paisley and with large windows that today were blurred by rain and fog. The smell of tea, lemons and coffee hung in the air. It was rather crowded, and there were a lot of people talking.

Regina and I plopped down into empty chairs across from Priya and Karan. "Hammy… Gina, we'd been dying to talk to you."

"Oh," I said, "What about?"

"We wanted to ask you what it was like living with a murderer? And Regina, you simply must tell us what it was like dating a murderer. I can't quite imagine if it would be chilling or thrilling… but you do seem the sort to be into that."

Regina's eyes darkened a fraction, "Whatever do you mean, Karan darling?"

"Oh, just that you are always so posh and perfect, aren't you? It makes sense that you would go for the bad boy type," Priya said, and she and Karan chuckled before he said, "So do tell us, Regina, did you know? Or was it a surprise?"

Regina pursed her pink lips, "Oh, I was quite surprised."

Her tone was like frosted glass, and so to avoid her leaping up on the table and pulling their hair, I steered the conversation over to the reason we had sat across the prickly pair in the first place.

"So, um, well, at my mother's Christmas party, you two said that you believed that you were the last people to see the Lady Moira Barking alive… what, um, what did you see exactly?"

Priya preened as she turned back to us, "Oh, it's all rather dramatic," she said.

Regina smiled, though her hands were gripping the straps of her red handbag so tight her knuckles blanched. "I don't suppose you could be persuaded to tell us?"

"We are most happy too," Karan said, "it is a rather exciting tale."

Priya leaned forward, "So, that summer Karan and I had taken it upon ourselves to practice our tennis in the park every morning, and as a reward we would get ourselves a little treat from that adorable little bakery on Drury Lane.

Karan took over, "So that day Priya ordered a saffron macchiato and I had a matcha latte… and we were chatting about this darling new tv show… what's it called? Oh yes, 'The Emerald Circle'. I think your Nicky's uncle is in it? Anyway, I so happened to look up, and there I spotted Lady Barking sitting by her lonesome on a two-person table."

Regina and I leaned in close, "Around what time was that?" she asked.

Priya and Karan turned to face each other, and she said, "Oh well…we met in the park at around ten. We finished our sets around eleven. We would have gotten to the bakery around 11:10… and we saw Her Grace around then."

Regina and I looked at each other for a long moment, only interrupted when Karan said, "Oh… and that's not even the most interesting part."

Regina whipped around, "There's more?"

Karan preened, "So, as we watched her, Lady Moira seemed to be waiting for someone. She kept checking her phone and casting glances at the door. And then suddenly, she looked out the window, stood up rather suddenly and left out the back door. The back door, mind you."

Regina was silent for a long moment, but after a moment, she said, "That is terribly interesting."

"Did you see who or what it was that spooked her so?" I asked, and the pair shook their heads.

"No," pouted Priya, "But not for lack of trying. We went over to the window immediately, and all we saw was an empty street."

Regina's eyes locked on me. After a moment, we excused ourselves from the table and walked back out into the rain, stopping under a gnarled tree for shelter. "Well, this certainly proves that the old witch didn't off herself."

I stared up at the dance of the rain on the leaves, "Who… who do you think she saw? Who was it that upset her so?"

"Well… I do not quite know. I guess we will just have to find out… I think we need to go to London… a talk with our dear friend Nicky is long since overdue"

Chapter Thirty-Four

Friday
9th February, 2024

Football practice had been called off because of a rather bad storm, which I found a shame as I like playing in the rain, but the extra two hours of sleep were quite welcome. Biology class was interesting; we talked about the human heart. In geography, we had to memorise all the rivers of Europe, which actually went hand in hand with history because we talked about the battle at the River Vánagandr and the Sea Battles at Hormus during the third war.

Sir Hugh had also called off detention, but because Regina and I were headed to London tomorrow, we needed his permission and signature, and so I went to his office. His secretary, a very nice lady named Miss Tilly, told me he was meeting a student, but that since all I needed was a signature, I could steal a moment.

There was the sound of a girl's voice, and she sounded terribly upset. When I knocked, she fell silent and, after a moment, came Sir Hugh's voice rather gruffer than usual, "Come in."

Sir Hugh was sitting in his usual chair, and sitting across from him was none other than Electra Barking. Both of them were looking angry and frustrated, but Sir Hugh's face softened when he saw me, "Ah, Lord Hamlet, I thought you got my message. We shan't be meeting today."

I nodded, stepping into the office and taking out the form, "Yes, Sir, but Lady Regina De Winter and I plan to visit London this weekend, and we need your permission."

Electra Barking's eyes were downcast, and she didn't react to my presence, but Sir Hugh took the form from me, "Ah and might I ask what you will be doing in London?"

"We're going to visit Nicholas," I said, "We're both rather worried about him, Sir. And we thought he could do with some cheering up."

His face was grave. "Lady Electra, would you be so kind as to wait outside for a few moments?" Wordlessly, she rose to her feet and walked out the door. Once she was gone, he made an attempt at a smile. "How sweet of you both. How will you be getting to London?" he asked.

"Lady Regina has hired us a car for the day."

"Excellent. And where shall you be staying?"

"At my place in London, Sir, it's all there on the form."

"Very well, just making sure," he said, taking up a blue pen and scratching his signature across the required area.

"Can I ask you a question, Lord Hamlet?" he said, looking at me, and I nodded. "Do you believe Nicholas' confession?"

I swallowed, "I believe that he believes it. Though I believe that he is mistaken."

It had been on my tongue to mention the mix-up with the plants, but that would raise too many questions. "Truth be told, Sir, Regina and I seek to find out the truth."

His grey eyes bore into me, "A noble sentiment to be sure, but I would advise you to tread carefully. We are dealing with a very dangerous individual here. One won't shy away from any crime, no matter how foul it might be."

I met his gaze, "Sir, believe me, I know. This person came into my home under my mother's hospitality and murdered another guest. I am fully aware of how dangerous the person is."

He handed me back the form, "Lord Hamlet, again, please do tread carefully, this person might be far closer than you could imagine." I stared at him for a beat, and his eyes never left me, and all I could do was mutely nod. And he went on, "And if you do insist on investigating this, remember the motive for murder is always quite simple and always comes down to hatred, love, or greed."

I stared at him, reflecting on what an odd man he was. "Thank you, Sir."

He nodded and gave me leave, and so I stepped out and into the waiting area.

Electra sat there alone, and when she looked up at me, her face was rather red and blotchy. "You're quite alright, Electra?"

She stared at me, "Yes…yes… Drinkwater can be quite a stubborn man. He's quite so narrow-minded and hung upon his principles and antiquated sense of morality that it's hard to make him see sense about anything."

I sighed, "Yes. Well, I know. I did get stuck in detention for defending myself from your brother. But the old man is wiser than he seems."

She stared at me, "And what's this about you going to London? Going to visit a murderer, are you?"

"Electra," I said, "I was wrong about Nicholas. I don't think..."

She scowled. "Yes… Yes, my brother is always very good at convincing people of his innocence. He never gets into trouble for anything… even the things he did." And with that, she shoved past me and walked back into the office.

I watched her go, and then I walked back to the library. Regina sat there in our usual spot, going over biology notes about atriums and heart valves with Fiona. I handed her the form, and she put it neatly into a folder and slid it away into her bag. I have to admire her dedication to her files and folders. I just put things into my bag willy-nilly, but now she had separate folders for each subject and even one for field hockey.

Fiona frowned, "So, you are headed to London for the weekend? It shall get terribly dull without you."

"Oh, we know, darling," Regina said with a smile, "But we have some business to attend to. Can't be avoided, I am afraid."

Chapter Thirty-Five

Saturday, London
10th February, 2024

London was deep in the last throes of winter, and snow clung to the ground. Sounds charming, I know, but the snow was rather filthy and slushy and gushy beneath our feet. At the Thamesgate, the door was opened by none other than Lord Barking himself; he seemed momentarily shocked before he broke into a smile. "Ah, Hamlet and Lady Regina, what an unexpected delight." He eyed us for a moment before stepping aside, "Do come in out of the cold." A butler hurried over, relieving us of our coats. Lord Barking smiled at us, "It has been quite a while since I have had visitors. Shall we take tea in my study?"

Regina nodded imperiously, "Yes, please, I do love a good floral tea with two sugars and a dash of lemon."

She strolled past Lord Barking and up to the stairs, "However, I simply must pay a quick visit to Nicholas; poor darling must be pining away for me." Then, without wasting time or waiting for permission, she strolled up the stairs.

Lord Barking watched her in amusement, "I must say I was rather surprised when my son announced he had a girlfriend. Or rather, when the girlfriend announced herself… never saw Nicholas as having much of an interest in the fairer sex."

Regina froze for a moment, "Well, he does seem to prefer his books to people. But that was before I showed him flesh and blood make better companions than ink and paper." And with that, she walked up the stairs and out of sight.

Lord Barking gestured for me to follow him into his study, "She's a clever one that Regina De Winter… can't help but wonder where she got it from."

He sat down at his desk, staring at me, "Do you still like your tea the same way? Lots of milk, lots of sugar?"

I nodded, "I do, Harry."

He nodded, passing the instructions along to the butler. And then turned to me, "Hamlet, do you know how long I have held my position? By which I mean as CEO of Barkings News and as 'the spin doctor?' he asked rather out of nowhere.

I stared at him, "No, I do not."

"About twenty-two years now. I took it over when I was just a bit older than Electra. Back when the war was just beginning, and do you know what I did first?" he said, still staring at me over steepled fingers, and then, without waiting for a response, "This was when word of our country's and our allies' less than savoury actions in war were creeping in. So, what do we do?"

He stared at me, waiting for an answer, "Talk about the enemy? And their crimes?"

He nodded, "People want a war but not a dirty war. But war isn't won by honour and the Geneva Conventions. It is won by filth and blood. But people don't want to hear that. They want a hero to root for. So, what do we do? We give them one? We pick a random general or a random soldier, blow his deeds out of proportion and make him the face of the campaign. Turn him into an almost Arthurian figure. No matter what other blights he might have against his name. And then you dig through history, dragging up every single offence against us and our allies that the enemy has committed as far as living memory could feasibly stretch."

"You remind everyone of what they did during the war?" I suggested.

Lord Barking seemed to weigh this, "Well, yes, when the war is still fresh in everyone's minds. But people tire of war and blood. So, you distract with something a little more light-hearted. You divert the press and public with some harmless but scandalous tale about the lives of those they put on a pedestal, perhaps the Prince and Princess of Wales have fallen into rather unedifying habit of airing their dirty laundry on the Buckingham balcony… people love royalty… but they love royal gossip more."

I nodded, "Makes sense, I suppose. Follow the birdie and all that?"

He nodded a subtle smile on his pale face, "And what do you do when people start pointing fingers at us… at the elite?"

I didn't respond, and his smile deepened, "People are simple, Hamlet, they hate each other for such silly reasons. Use whatever imaginary boundaries and borders they believe in. Turn them against each other. Make them think all their problems are because of the mythic other, and you have them eating out of your hand. It is a tried and tested tactic. Divide and conquer. Been employed by every government in the world for centuries."

"Why do you think I am telling you all this, Hamlet?" he asked. The butler had brought in the tea, and Lord Barking handed me my cup, but not before stirring in my sugar for me. I stared at him, trying to figure out what exactly the point of all this was, "A history lesson perhaps?"

Lord Barking laughed, "No, my son. I live and breathe truths, half-truths and narratives. Why, I spin stories for a whole nation for a living. It's what the Barkings have done for centuries. I mean to show you that it is rather pointless to lie to me. I have known you your whole life, Hamlet. I can read you. So, tell me… why have you and Lady Regina shown up at my door out of the blue?"

"You and my mother are together," I said, and Lord Barking's face went from shock to composed in the blink of an eye.

"No point in lying, I suppose," he mused in an amused tone, "How did you figure it out?"

I smiled, "I do have eyes, Harry."

And he smiled, "Clever boy. I suppose you must feel rather betrayed, but believe your mother and I are very much in love, and…"

"I know," I said, "And I don't feel betrayed. In a way, I think I have always known."

After a moment, I frowned, "Might I ask a question?" And he nodded. "Why did you and Mother not marry? If you two were very much in love, surely it would have been better to marry right off the bat, and avoid all the lies and cheating?"

He smiled a little sadly, "Well, we had broken up. Took us too long to come to our senses."

I finished my tea. "Might I talk to Nicholas?" He nodded, "Certainly."

I headed up the stairs and towards the bedroom. I knocked and opened the door. Nicholas sat on the bed, and Regina sat in a chair. I walked over, gave Nicholas a handshake and then slapped him slightly on the cheek. "That…" I said, ignoring his whining, "…was for bringing your little detective into my home. And for groping your impious hands around my terrarium."

Regina raised an eyebrow and smirked, "So anyway, Nicky, why don't you tell Hamlet what you told me?" Nicholas, still rubbing his cheek (it was a harmless tap, I tell you), protested till Regina shot him a look and he quelled.

"She didn't kill herself," Nicholas said more to himself.

"How do you know?" I asked softly.

"She wouldn't have left Electra and me," Nicholas said, "not by choice… and that day she was heading to an appointment. She had her clothes all ironed and ready, and she had gone for a bath."

Nicholas' gaze was locked on a spot on the floor. "She was headed to meet Jenny Leach," he said, "I found it in her calendar."

There was a moment of silence. He went on, "I think my mother was going to have Jenny follow your mum and my dad around. Get some proof, maybe for blackmail or something. And she winds up dead the very same day, and the private investigator winds up dead six months later."

I stared at Nicholas "So… why do you think you killed Miss Smith?"

Nicholas gaze didn't leave the floor, "Remember when you showed me your terrariums? One of the plants in there was hemlock. I took some and slipped it into her mead."

I turned to Regina, "Well, the funny thing is. Even if he had allowed her to drink it, she would have been fine," I said, smirking up at Nicholas, "Nicholas might know his books, but I know my plants.

That was Queen Anne's lace. At most, he would have given her wine a mild carroty flavour."

Regina chuckled, "You have got to be kidding. Oh, well, I suppose that says something about the competence of men."

Nicholas eyes shone in the golden light coming from the streets. "Are you sure?"

I smiled, "Positive."

He went silent, and after a moment, he swallowed, "Can I show you both something?"

We nodded, and Nicholas stood up and motioned for us to follow him, and we did. He led us down a long, dark hallway and to a closed door. He silently turned the brass doorknob, and the door swung open.

It was an elegant bedroom with marble fittings and a lace-covered four-poster bed. "Oh dear Nicholas," Regina said, and her voice was barely a whisper. I found myself unable to tear my gaze away from the shadows of the room; every little detail seemed to burn in my mind. The chess-like back and checkered flooring, the yellow glint of the wall sconces, the thick curtains that draped the wall on the other end of the room, no doubt obscuring a window. The framed faces on the wall are now covered in dust. The air had a horrible, cold stillness to it, and I wondered what the room looked like on that day.

Nicholas wordlessly stepped into the room, went to the curtains and drew them back. Through the window, one could see the snow-laden street and the park across, some of the streetlight filtered through the barren tree limbs, casting dancing shadows onto Nicholas' pale face. It faced the park, which meant this room was at the back of the house.

Regina and I followed him into the room, and I felt so very rigid, holding my hands close against my body, as though touching anything would somehow afflict or curse me. Nicholas studied us in silence for a moment, "On that day... the day my mother died. She'd hung her dress from there," he said, indicating a hook on the wall just to the right of the large wardrobe. "And she'd had her makeup box set up on her desk," he said. "And what's more... this window was wide open," he said, jabbing a thumb at the glass. "It would not be impossible to climb the wall. It was a wet, rainy day, and there weren't many people on the streets. And… the trees were in full bloom, which means the wall would have been obscured… which means that…"

"A person could theoretically climb up and down the wall without being seen," Regina said, "But Nicholas, you do realise that surely your mother would have raised some sort of alarm if she'd come in and seen a person here?

Nicholas pointed at the curtains, "These curtains could easily obscure even an adult standing behind them. Perhaps she didn't see him or her until it was too late."

Regina bit her lip, "You know Priya and Karan told us they saw your mother at Belle's Bakery, and your mother seemed spooked and ran out the door… hours before she was killed."

I was thinking of odd little things people had said to me over the past few months; of little lies and inconsistencies. I remembered the grin of the crumbling gargoyle. "Someone was very invested in us not having this conversation," I said at last. "Divide and conquer and all that."

Both Regina and Nicholas looked up at me, "Whatever do you mean, darling?"

I sighed, that would have been a lovely moment for a grand reveal, but I didn't have more than an inkling… yet. "I am not sure," I confessed, "But… well, almost am. I just need a few final pieces."

Nicholas rolled his eyes, "Wonderful… you think yourself a Poirot. Going to start referring to yourself in third person now, Rook?

I sighed, "Droll as ever, Barking, but do start paying attention. Someone at school has a very vested interest in you thinking you're the murderer and in the rest of us believing you."

His levity died a little, "I know… I know…"

He was quiet again, "I was thinking all of these things all this time. And I was so, so angry. And, on the day of the funeral, that man came up to me. He said he had been friends with Mum when they were at the academy together. That he had introduced her to Jenny Leach, he also introduced me to Miss Leach…"

Regina frowned, "That man?"

I stared out into the London fog as it swirled up and down the almost deserted street. A lone figure stood under the streetlamp, barely illuminated by the warm yellow glow. I had a sneaking suspicion. "The one from the party," Nicholas whispered to Regina as they stared at the cold, clean bed, "David Monroe."

Chapter Thirty-Six

"I need some fresh air." I walked out before she could question me and went down the darkened stairs and out the door and into the cold.

David Monroe stood alone, his dark blond hair catching the glint of the streetlamp. I walked up towards him, the wind nipping at my cheeks and my nose. "Mr Monroe," I said when I reached him.

"Ah, you remember me," he said with the smile of a serpent,

I stared up at him, "I remember you made quite a scene, and Mother had you thrown out into the snow," I said.

His face darkened for the spasm of a second, and then he chuckled, "Ah, yes… that was quite dramatic, Ham. Do you remember what I wanted back then?"

I stared at him for a long moment, "Something about my aunt?"

He stepped a little closer to me, "Indeed. Your aunt and I were together when we were at the academy, you know? I loved her then, and I love her still. And she still loves me."

I stared up at him, and I remembered what Delilah Stormwater-Keyne had said. "Been talking to her? Did you have a séance?"

His smile did not falter, "Oh no, Ham. I have no need of seances." He ended the word with a secretive sort of smile, almost as though he was sharing an inside joke. "Before I forget," he said, handing me a wrapped parcel vaguely in the shape of a book. "What is it?" I asked.

David seemed to relax slightly, "You will see… but you will find it enlightening, I assure you, and there will be another after this one. This world, Hamlet, we have buried it under concrete and steel, but the old world still lives, and that," he pointed, "will open it up for you."

I looked at him and then back at the trees, but I slipped the parcel into my pocket, "The old world? Do you mean to say she was the superstitious sort?"

He smiled, "What they call superstition, we call the truth. It's all true... old stories... the gods... the faeries... all of it."

I stared at him, wondering if I was in the company of a madman. "You mean like Zeus? Odin? All that lot?"

He smiled, "No, no, those are the new gods. The ones I speak of have no name. Come with me... just give me half an hour. Please?"

My curiosity warred with my self-preservation, but as usual, my nosiness won out. We walked in silence through snowy streets, coming to a townhouse on the other side of the park. He let me in, and the first thing I noticed was that there were no light bulbs or lamps. He must have seen my confusion, for he said, "I do not hold with artificial light. It damages the soul."

Suddenly, a floorboard creaked in the darkness above, and I looked up. "Who is that?"

David smiled, "You know who..." And his voice trailed off. He gestured at the stairs. And for some reason, probably because I am deeply stupid, I walked up the stairs, and David followed. The first floor was dark and empty, as was the ground floor, and David led me into a room.

He gestured to a chair, and I remained standing. "We're alone... whom did I hear?"

He ignored my question, pouring himself a measure of whiskey which he downed in a single shot, "You know, as incredible as it might seem, your mother, Harry, and I were all very good friends in those days."

He stared out at the inky black of the sky as the rain pattered down on his window, "Do you know why they all hate me? Why am I no longer welcome in their little world?"

"I imagine it has something to do with the fact that you're not the most agreeable of people, shall we say?"

David chuckled darkly, a sound that felt less human and more like something feral "I'd expected that... and I suppose it's true. But the true answer..." he said, "is that they thought me lower, because my father wasn't a lord of business. He was the groundskeeper on the Rook estate. My mother was a maid in your house."

For a moment, the intense anger that always seemed to simmer behind his handsome features faded away, and he seemed decades younger, almost like an insecure boy. "Your grandfather was many, many things, but he did so love control. As an apparent reward for my parents, he paid for me to attend that academy. I was excited, really. 'The opportunity of a lifetime,' my mother said."

He chuckled again, a deep, low sound, "The other kids were not very welcoming. Thought I was forcing myself into their world. That I had ideas above 'my station'. And so they punished me, picking on… picking fights but only in groups and never one on one."

He turned from the window, his gaze locking onto mine, "They hated me because I wasn't like them. They saw me as an outsider in their perfect world. And I tried at first to be like them… I dressed like them, talked like them, walked like them. I followed all their rules, protocols and hierarchies. I spent money I didn't have to show them I could. And what I couldn't earn in summer jobs scrubbing toilets, I stole." His lips twisted into a smile that didn't reach his eyes. "Dahlia joined in soon. She had no reason to. Your grandparents gave her anything she asked for. She stole for the thrill of it. I realised then the difference between us… she could steal and get away with it. It became a game for us."

He went on, seeming to forget I was there, "I realised then, why force myself into a world that doesn't want me? When I can remake it to fit me. I looked around at all those proud, pampered faces. And, I asked myself… what do kids…what do people like this desire above all else?"

He looked at me, as though expecting an answer. And somehow I knew it at once, and I muttered, "Freedom… and no consequences."

His chuckle was a low rumbly thing, "Exactly… they spent all their lives in their posh little palaces. Minding their Qs and Ps and dotting their 'Is' and crossing their 'Ts'. Turning into mini versions of their parents. They were never really allowed to just let loose. Engage in unrestrained pleasure. So that's what we gave them – Dahlia, Delilah and me."

The rain outside intensified, the sound of it pounding against the glass as if in response to his words. David's smirk was feral, like a fallen angel cast down from grace, unrepentant and proud.

I swallowed hard, trying to keep up, my thoughts scrambling like frightened mice. "But… rules… are… aren't all that bad," I stammered, "I mean, they keep us safe."

He chuckled darkly, a sound like distant thunder. "Safe? Safe from who, exactly? Ourselves? The only thing these rules protect us from is what we're truly meant to be. They don't keep us safe; they keep us small."

I blinked, my voice small in comparison. "Well, I meant murderers and killers…"

David threw his head back and laughed, "You think rules stop them?" His grin was feral. "The innocent are punished, and the guilty walk free? In the old world, murderers, thieves – they'd be hanged for all to see. Not 'rehabilitated,' not coddled. Justice, back then, was swift and true."

I could feel the heat rising in my cheeks, struggling to find the right words. "But—"

He cut me off, his voice a sharp blade. "And what about now? These same rules you cling to so desperately? They let the homeless die on the streets, kicked out of empty buildings like trash. They let wealth rot in the hands of the few while the many starve. Every day, new insults slap the face of heaven… so how are your rules helping anyone?" I had no answer. My lips moved, but nothing came out.

"There is no but, Hamlet," he said, "This world of order, of 'laws' and 'rules'… It's a rotting corpse. It stinks of decay and fear. Your aunt knew it. I know it. And deep down, you know it."

I hated his words; they were like mould creeping in where it was not wanted. Poisoning my thoughts, making me think of things and remember things I didn't want to. I remembered passing homeless men and women in the streets and not even noticing them, too busy talking with Regina or my phone to notice. And then I would go home and barely touch whatever dinner was made.

I didn't say anything, but David did, "Dahlia saw… she saw what all the rest of your mother's ilk ignored and spat on. She saw the rot and canker of the world, of wealth and privilege, your lot wear like perfume. She wanted to burn it all down, and they hated her for it."

"What do… what do the old gods have to do with it?" I managed through my dry throat, the weight of his words pressing on me like a dark cloud.

David's eyes glinted with a cold fire, and he leaned forward, "Everything, my boy, everything," he said. "It was your aunt who met him first… she told us of a stranger under the trees. She said he wasn't a true stranger, as she'd known him her whole life."

"What does that mean?" I asked, he didn't answer, but he stood slowly turning toward the window, his silhouette framed by the rain-soaked glass. "You should go now," he said quietly, "your friends are waiting for you."

Chapter Thirty-Seven

"How crazy are you!" Regina muttered when I was back in Barking Manor. "What on earth possessed you to walk off with a stranger, without so much as a by your leave?"

Nicholas sighed, "It was rather rude… if you got murdered, my father would never let me hear the end of it," he said, frowning at me.

I rolled my eyes, "Touched by your concern... really."

"Anyway," Regina had said, "Listen. Now that we sorted out who is not the killer, we need to figure out who the killer actually is."

I nodded, glancing sideways at Nicholas, "And we do know who the traitor is. I must say I am a little disappointed."

He cast a grim grin, "Were you expecting a conspiracy?"

Regina interrupted, "I do suppose figuring out how our murderous friend got in and out of a locked room would be the first step. Perhaps this person was someone known to Miss Leach? She let them in of her own accord?"

"You know," Nicholas said, "I think myself more of a Poirot."

"Why? Because you also have a million little eccentricities?"

"No, Rook," he said, "Because I am more of the armchair sort. But I do suppose someone needs to do the legwork." I rolled my eyes, and he chuckled.

Regina rolled her eyes fondly, "Anyway, Nicky darling… do tell us why exactly you confessed… what was in those letters you were ranting and raving about."

His face darkened, "Well, just what I said. Ever since the party, I've been getting… letters threatening to tell Father what I thought I did, unless I followed their demands." Regina's gaze lingered on me for a moment. "What sort of demands?"

Nicholas didn't meet our gaze; he stared at his hands, picking numbly at the skin around his nails, "Nothing major… at first. It was a demand for money. Nothing major, mind you, just five pounds or ten pounds, I had to leave in specified spots around the school. I suppose whoever it was just wanted to prove that they could intimidate me."

I stared at him for a long moment, "Anything else?"

He nodded, still not looking at us, "Yes… other small things. I had to cut my hair… things to show I was under control… that kind of thing. I had enough eventually, and well, I confessed."

Regina and I exchanged a long look. "Well," she said at last, "Enough of that. Whoever this person is, they were just… playing a cruel little game."

I nodded, "Did you keep any of the letters, Barking? We might be able to identify the handwriting, perhaps?"

He shook his head, "No… I burned them all. I was angry and frustrated and…."

Regina and I exchanged a look, and I sighed, "Very well… never mind then. But enough of this self-pity, Barking, you're coming back with us tomorrow."

He almost smiled, but then went sullen, "But I don't see my father letting me out anytime soon."

Regina smiled, "We shall simply have to see about that."

Regina and I talked to Lord Harry, and I explained to him about the flowers and the awful mix-up. Regina promised to keep Nicholas on best behaviour. Nicholas merely sat there in silence.

Lord Barking sighed, "Very well. You may return to school, Nicholas. But if you step even the fraction of an inch out of line…." He left the threat hanging.

Nicholas merely nodded and left the room. Lord Barking stared from me to Regina, He smiled, "I do hope you two find the killer…"

He rose smiling magnanimously, "You are both welcome to spend the night here, of course. I have business in New York. I shall be taking an early flight. When I return, I expect the name of the killer and proof."

"And you shall have it, your Grace," I said, and then, after a moment, "My first football game is coming up soon. I shall be quite touched if you were to attend."

He was silent for a moment, and then he smiled. "Then I shall be there." He'd made to leave, but I called out.

"Lord Barking? Do you happen to know a couple by the name of Lord and Lady Greenwood?"

He froze in place, and there was some unreadable emotion in his face, and for a moment it seemed like fear. "No," he said at last, "I can't say I do." He seemed on the verge of saying something else, but then he turned and left with a "Goodnight, son."

The next day, we left London when it was still rising from its sleep, and the streets were empty. I stared out of the window, watching as the city rolled away and the people grew scarcer. Nicholas had fallen back asleep with his head resting against the window. Regina sat in silence, her green eyes reflecting the passing world.

It was snowing outside, and the snow turned to rain against the windows. As we drove, we passed houses, trees and people. A stranger under the trees?

I tapped her knee, "Regina, do you believe in the old stories?" There was a moment of confused silence, and I patted myself on the back for being able to stump Regina De Winter. "What do you mean?" she asked.

"My aunt… she and David met someone he called the stranger who lived in the trees," I whispered over the wind howling outside.

"You mean like some sort of lunatic living in the woods?

"Well… not like some derelict destitute but like well like— "

"Like what?" she interrupted impatiently."

"Like a spirit or a ghost. Ridiculous, isn't it?" I said, laughing awkwardly. "But I have this memory. I must have been around four. I had been playing with a ball in the garden. I had wandered off, and I lost my ball in the woods. I got myself lost looking for it. It was getting dark, and I was getting scared, and then a man seemed to appear out of the trees for a moment right before Mother found me." I said. "I had told mother, and while she coddled me and scolded me for running off, she looked around and assured me it was just my own imagination."

"Hamlet," she said suddenly, "Do you remember this from when we were about eight? Our mothers had been sitting down to tea, and we begged for ten more minutes to play rather insistently until they relented. They then insisted that it be only ten minutes and they would be timing us," she said in a voice as soft as summer grass.

"I remember… it was you, me. Colin and Wendy… we dashed into the old woods to our rather sorry excuse of a treehouse. We played knights and dragons or something, and we played for hours. We played until it got dark, and then we ran home terrified that they would yell at us…"

She was even softer, "And when we got out it was broad summer sunlight and your mother said, "Oh my… back and with three minutes to spare.' We felt like it had been hours… they said minutes."

I didn't quite meet her eyes. "Anyway, as you said, let's not let our imagination get away with us."

"Quite right," she said, and we held each other's gaze for a very long moment. Nicholas scowled at us for disturbing his nap, and so we spent the rest of the drive in silence.

We returned to campus quite late. The island's air was sweet and salty. Regina returned to her room, craving a hot shower, but after the long drive, I needed to stretch my legs, so Nicholas and I went for a walk. It wasn't raining, but it certainly was about to. The sky was grey, and there was a distinct bite in the air.

"Barking? Do you believe in gods and ghosts?" I said as we walked along the spitting sea. Nicholas's hands were in his pockets, and rain droplets plastered his hair to his face.

Out on the foggy sea, orbs of light danced, and I grabbed Nicholas' arm and pointed, "Look." He stared out at the lights and then turned to me, "Those are ships, Rook. You know they're like big cars that can swim."

I didn't respond. Nicholas stared out at sea for another moment and then, quietly, he turned and walked away, "Let's go back, Rook."

Colin, Arch, Duffy and Windsor were all lounging around. When Nicholas and I walked past, they all did a perfect double-take in unison. "Hang on," Archie said, "What's he doing here? Didn't he kill someone?"

"No," I said, dropping my bag onto my bed, "Long story."

Colin groaned, watching as Nicholas wheeled his suitcases back into their rightful place, "Well… hang on… didn't he confess?"

I sat on my bed, kicking off my shoes, "Yes, but he got confused. You understand. It is Barking… he can't tell his head from the other end."

Chapter Thirty-Eight

Monday
12th February, 2024

Well, today Sir Hugh wasn't on campus, and so we didn't have detention. My lunch hour was free, but sadly, it wasn't to be spent in leisure as Regina De Winter had other plans. We realised we needed to speak to a potential witness. Rowan De Winter answered the FaceTime call, and his mouth was coated with Cheeto dust. And as always, he held the phone far too close to his face for comfort, "Hello, hello," I said.

" 'Lo…" he said, annoyed as though we interrupted him doing something terribly important. Regina cleared her throat, "Rowan, dear. Do have the good grace to look at us when we're talking to you."

He scowled vaguely at her, "I am in the middle of a particularly intense round, Gina, what do you want?"

Regina opened her mouth, but I shushed her, "Sorry to bother you, Rowan, but we have something we need to ask you. Do you remember the night of the party… the night that woman fell? Did you see or hear anything odd?"

He was silent for a long moment, and there was the sound of video game violence before he spoke, "Well. There was a scream."

"Yes," Regina said impatiently, "We all heard the scream. Did you hear anything? You were sitting by the mudroom door. Did anyone other than us enter or leave at all?"

He frowned suddenly, and his game went silent as he paused it. He picked up his phone, "Now that you mention it. When I was waiting for you to return, there was a rather loud, well, it wasn't a knock, but more like someone throwing themselves against the door. I thought it was one of you... And when I opened the door, there was no one there, and then you lot showed up moments later."

Regina and I exchanged a look. Rowan shook his head, "What are you two up to? Why all these questions?"

Regina sighed, "Nothing you need to worry about, Rowan, do your homework, wash your face, and get off your Xbox."

He narrowed his eyes at us for a moment before he sighed, "Fine. Miss you both," and with that, he hung up.

Nicholas sighed, "Your family is ever so charming, De Winter."

I turned to Regina, "If the killer couldn't access the mudroom… the front door was locked and bolted too…"

"What are you thinking?"

I nodded, "Well, I have a question that I need to ask a certain prince."

"What question might that be?" Regina demanded

"Oh, darling," I said, "That would give away the game.

The next morning at football practice, we ran the usual drills, had a practice, and after the huddle, we all went off for breakfast. Windsor had forgotten his change of clothes in his room and so headed back, and I followed, sensing the opportunity.

"So, Windsor," I said as we fell into step. "I have a question."

Windsor half turned as we backed to the towers, "What's up, Rook?"

"Remember a few weeks ago you told us that Lord Barking brought a petition before the royal court seeking to attaint Nicholas as his heir?" I asked.

He nodded with a slight, "Yes. Why do you ask?"

I went on, "Do you remember that you said that in order for one to attain their trueborn son and heir, it is no simple matter?" I asked, "Well, what would that process be like?"

He shrugged, "Well. The easiest option would be for him to surrender his rights, but should he refuse, he would have to be found unworthy, then he could be disinherited or attainted by a decree."

I stopped, and he stopped too. "And what would the process of getting that decree be?"

He seemed confused by the question, but he answered, "Well, first, a formal petition the lord or lady would need to submit a formal petition to the crown. And they would need a valid reason for disinheriting the heir. If the crown finds this sufficient, the degree would be granted, and a new heir would be named."

I stared up at him and asked, "What would be considered a sufficient reason?"

Windsor frowned, "Well, madness, a poor moral compass, health problems, or perhaps—"

"If the heir was found to be guilty of a crime. A serious crime, mind you," I said, "such as murder. Would that be sufficient reason to attain him?"

I knew the answer. Windsor nodded, "Yes, there is a precedent for it. In 1856, Lord Quagmire's heir was found guilty of murdering a scullery maid. So his daughter was made heir. Before that, in 1492…" He went on for quite a bit. Old Windsor loves history. But I already had my answer. All that was left to do was catch the killer.

I walked with him back to the tower and waited while he got his stuff, and then we went off to breakfast together. Classes went well, in business and politics, we had our proposals due, which of course I did excellently in, we Rooks do have a natural affinity for these things.

In the afternoon, I had detention with Sir Hugh. He looked up through his glasses, "Well, Lord Hamlet, hello…"

"Hello," I said.

"I won't be asking how you managed to convince Harry to release Nicholas, but if you do wish to tell me, I won't stop you," he said, setting down the newspaper he'd been reading.

"Well, that would be telling, Sir," I said with a smirk. He rolled his eyes fondly, and I cleared my throat, "You told me that the motive for murder is always quite simple: love, hatred and greed."

Sir Hugh was silent for a long moment. "Yes."

I sat in my chair, "Hatred, I understand; people kill for hate all the time, I see it on the news. Greed, I understand one might kill for an…"

"An inheritance?" he provided, looking at me over steepled fingers. And in that gesture, he looked so much like Mother or like Lord Barking that I almost laughed. I wondered if they picked it up from him.

"Yes," I said, "But I don't understand how one can kill for love."

He sat back in his chair, "Well, one might kill to protect a loved one, for instance or look at the case of Macbeth, he killed his king out of both love and greed. His greed for power and his love for his wife."

"Must you tie everything into Shakespeare, Sir?" I said.

"Well," he said with a smile, "Shakespeare's stories are timeless because he was a master of human relationships; he had it all figured out 500 years ago. Language may change, styles of dress may change, forms of government might change, but people stay the same. Motive stays the same."

"I suppose you are right about that."

His face was suddenly grave, "Although I will allow that there are some exceptions," he said in a voice barely above a whisper, "Some just kill for the pleasure in taking a life. For the feeling of power and for the apparent beauty in barbarism."

Before I could say anything, Nicholas walked in with apologies for his tardiness, and so we went on with the lesson.

Later, I found my way to the library to sit and wait. It was a cold, rainy day, the sort that dispels plans of cricket or football and finds us sitting in the library. I perched myself on one of the cosy armchairs before the hearth. Nicolas was sitting in the opposite armchair, and after a polite conversation had lapsed into silence. I found myself studying the pale, elegant lines of his face; I had noticed that when at rest, his face takes on a sort of brooding expression. It suited him immensely. "Nicholas," I whispered, feeling almost guilty at disturbing his serene solitude, "I have a question I need to ask."

He half looked up from his book, "Go on."

I stared at him, not sure how to broach this subject, "Your father sought to attaint you as his heir. You would have been stripped of your title."

He was silent for a moment and then said, "Oh yes. I know… he thought I didn't, but I did. My mother… she always came to the defence. There was a great deal of noise about it. I was quite upset about it at the time."

I frowned at him, "Are you not anymore?"

He gave a bitter laugh, "Rook. I have since lost my mother, thought a murderer, and been placed under house arrest by my own father. What does a title mean? It's just vanity beyond a point."

"I suppose you're right," I said, "Well, it's just that I am rather fond of mine."

He shrugged. And I asked my next question, "How did you find out?"

"Well, my parents' screaming matches on the matter made it rather hard not to know." We met each other's gaze, and we both fell into silence. "Nicholas," I said, "it was Electra."

His face went a whiter shade of pale, "W—what?"

I watched his face as I explained everything, going from anger to reluctant understanding, and he sighed, "Oh,"

"I am sorry," I said. He simply nodded mutely. His fingers tapped on his book, "Well... what are we going to do about it?"

Chapter Thirty-Nine

Tuesday
13th February, 2024

Well, today I caught a killer, and I got lightly stabbed. Let me tell you how it went. First, I found Regina, and when I got her and Nicholas together, I told her everything. We made a plan together. It struck me just how odd it was that I was planning to lay a trap for a killer with Nicholas Barking of all people on God's green earth.

Electra wasn't at polo practice the previous day, but I managed to get hold of her at breakfast in the morning. I asked if we could talk that night, perhaps on a walk in the woods? She'd smiled and nodded, "Oh, that does sound so romantic, Rook. How about the polo field? It's so quiet there after sunset, and we shall have plenty of privacy… say eight o'clock?" And so it was set.

The rest of the day passed in a blur, and I was rather distracted, but eventually night came, and then at 7:50, I walked over to the polo field and waited. She was late, but she came tossing down her blanket into the grass. "Hello, Rook," she said with the smile of a serpent.

She lowered herself onto her blanket, and it struck for the hundredth time just how gorgeous she was. She peered at me with those winter blue eyes, "I think we respect each other enough to skip the crap. Tell me, Rook, how did you work out that I killed Miss Piggy?"

"Why did you call her that?" A twig snapped in the darkness, and it took all my force of will not to look.

"Am I supposed to honour her with a name?" She scoffed, "What name might that be? Miss Kitty or Miss Leach?"

I held her gaze, "You know about that?"

She laughed, "Of course I do. She and Nicholas weren't very good at lies. All that yarn about homeschooling. I will admit the letter was very well forged. Even fooled father at first."

"He knew about her?"

She nodded, "He knew she wasn't who she claimed to be. I concede it was his roster of sleuths that discovered her identity. I think he imagined she was sent by some enemy from outside the family. Mind you, had he actually spent a moment thinking about his own children, he'd have found his little traitor very close to home."

"Is that why you killed her?"

"Well," Electra shrugged, "Yes and no. I would have killed her either way. She had designs on my father. Silly old woman had ideas above her station. Swanning around my house, acting like the lady of the manor. You can hardly fault me."

"But I can fault you for framing your brother," I said, shrugging at her.

Her laugh was violent and boisterous, "Oh, please. Nicholas is an idiot. He brought that woman into our world to spy on your mother and my father. I rather did you a favour."

I stared at her, "You didn't do it for me or your father or my mother. You did it for the title. You knew if your father and the King and his court thought Nicholas guilty, that would be sufficient grounds for him to be attainted, and you would be named heir and get the whole bloody thing… all for greed."

She cocked her head, evidently impressed, "My, my, you are smarter than you look. But again, you can't fault me and don't tell me you wouldn't kill for your birthright. I am older. The Barking title should be mine. It's only due to the shape of his genitals that he is the heir and not me," her voice began rising like the first low growl of a dog about to pounce, "Besides all that. Nicholas is an idiot; he can't manage a business. He doesn't deserve to be the Duke of London. I do. It should be mine."

"Is that why you killed his cat?" I asked.

She laughed again, "No… that was just for fun. I'd asked Mother for a dog for years, and she refused, but as soon as her delicate darling wanted a cat, she got him one. It was an annoying, loud thing anyway," she said, shrugging her slender shoulders.

"Well," she said, "Well then, darling, my turn for a question. How did you figure out I killed Piggy?"

"Barney… he broke up with his girlfriend at the start of the month. You lied about your alibi," I said, "And then you grabbed Nicky's wrist at dinner. That was when you stole the cufflink, wasn't it? I suppose now, in all the chaos at dinner, no one noticed you sneak off."

She shrugged, "I do suppose I have been rather careless. And here I thought myself a criminal genius. Anything else?"

"You hid under her bed, didn't you?"

She shook her head, "You lose one mark there, Rook. I hid in the closet. As soon as she said she wanted to go to her room, I knew the time was ripe. I slipped up the back staircase. I waited and peaked through the slit in the door."

"Then, after you did the deed, you climbed down the trellis. You were the only lady at the party not wearing a dress. The only one who could have managed such a climb in the snow and in the pitch dark."

She shrugged, "It was rather daring. You should be impressed, Rook."

"I would be, but you did attack me."

"Oh, c'mon, be a sport. I had no choice," she said, leaning back a little into the cold, damp grass.

"What about your many attempts on my life?" I asked, "The gargoyle?"

She gave me a slight pout, "Now, in my defence, I thought you caught a glimpse of my face when I attacked you. It was merely self-preservation… Anything else? I want to be prepared for my next murder."

"You were the only one it could have been," I said, "I realised it couldn't have been a parent after the first few attempts on my life... it had to be someone on campus. All of my classmates were in the greenhouse with us, so that excluded them. So that left you."

She nodded imperiously, "Anything else?"

She rose to her feet, taking slow steps toward me.

"Just one more thing," I said. I remained standing still, letting her come to me, "On the first day of classes, you mentioned 'the woman murdered' at the party, but the official police investigation said that she'd wandered off on her own. But word choice is everything, isn't it? You wanted me to think it was murder… to point me towards Nicholas."

She smiled faintly, her face luminous in the moonlight, "Here, I thought myself cunning. Oh well… I suppose now your little friend and my baby brother can come out of their hiding places."

A moment of tense silence, and slowly, Regina and Nicholas stepped out of the shadows.

Nicholas' face was moon white, and he was staring at Electra in silence. She stretched and said, "You know this was great fun. Confessing does feel rather good, not that any of it matters in any way."

Regina frowned, "Nicholas, Hamlet and I witnessed your confession, darling. Do you imagine we shall be keeping silent about it?

Electra sighed, "No. I expect you three shall blab to all the known world. If I let you live, that is!" She produced a knife, and its wicked blade caught the moonlight.

She turned to her brother with a smile that was more a baring of teeth, "How does a double murder-suicide sound?" She toyed with the blade, "You know if you die, I inherit. Should have thought of that years ago… drowned you in the tub as a baby or knocked you off your bike in the park… would've saved me all this fuss. But, oh well, better *late than never*!" and she lunged and slashed at her brother. Nicholas had frozen in place, but mercifully, Regina was swift on her feet, leaping backwards and pulling Nicholas by the collar. He stumbled backwards and fell.

I realised I should probably do something, so I pushed Electra, and it did very little, but she turned, slashing the blade towards me. I was a second too late, and pain split across my forearm. Regina was upon her, gripping and grasping at hair and limb. I grabbed Electra's blade arm and tried to pry the blade free, all the while she was howling like a mad wolf.

Electra was strong and swift, and she ripped herself free of us; her hair was wild, and she looked mad. She slashed again, and Regina and I leapt backwards in unison. My feet caught, and I fell hard, and Electra came down upon me, but I threw up the blanket. Regina grabbed me by the shoulder and pulled me up. And away we ran.

I grabbed a polo mallet someone had left behind as we passed, and we fled out onto the beach. And with a howl of hellish fury, Electra had ripped free of the blanket and was after us. I was very glad that my football practice and Regina's hockey practice started with a run on the beach, because we flew across the sand.

Or we did, until Nicholas tripped and we, being the compassionate people we were, stopped. Electra came out of the darkness, wielding her dagger and shrieking like some Spartan banshee. I swung the polo mallet, and she intercepted it with the knife. We crossed the blade and mallet again for a minute. Before Regina leapt upon her back in an aggressive piggyback ride. Electra slashed at Regina's arm and swung her off. Regina fell bleeding into the sand, but was already back on her feet. I threw a fistful of sand into Electra's eye, and we bolted up and away from the beach into the tree line.

All three of us were panting wildly, and Nick stumbled onto all fours, coughing and writhing. Blood was soaking my sleeve and seeping into the forest floor. Regina stood shaking like a leaf, her own blood mingled with mine on grass and detritus.

Electra flew through the trees behind us. Her arm lashed out, grabbing me by the collar, pulling me towards her, and the knife was raised high, and at that moment, there was an almighty crack. A heavy limb fell from a tree, and it caught Electra by the shoulder and fell down hard. Regina moved like lightning, grabbing up the blade, and her foot came down, pinning Electra to the ground.

We stood there in silence, all of us panting. "Now, now," Electra said, breaking the silence and raising her arms in surrender, "Let's not get hasty."

Regina dug her heel in deeper and hefted the blade, "Oh no, darling, let's!"

Oh, come on," Electra pouted, "You aren't going to kill me? All this over that little... incident?"

"Incident be damned," Regina whispered, "You just tried to kill Hamlet and me."

"Oh. What's a little murder between friends?"

Regina lifted the blade into the air, and Electra held up her hands placatingly, "Now, now, before you make a fool of yourself… listen." Regina faltered, "You have thirty seconds."

Electra nodded, "I shan't need more. First of all, I am sorry. Secondly, even if you do tell my father, what outcome do you expect? He isn't going to throw me into a prison cell."

I shrugged, holding my bleeding forearm. "He can drown you in the Thames for all I care."

"And what good would that do anyone?"

"I shall sleep sweeter," I said.

Now," Electra said, "What if we make a deal?"

Regina's laugh was almost a snarl, "Oh, you know what? I am curious, let's hear it, darling."

Electra's smile didn't waver, "Keep my secret, and I'll keep yours."

The knife dipped for a fraction of a moment, "I don't have any secrets."

"No," said Electra, "But your parents do. Remember all those nasty accusations that man was making? They're all quite true. And Miss Piggy had proof of them all. And her proof now rests with me. Keep my secret, and those secrets stay buried."

I watched Regina meet Electra's eyes, and we both saw that Electra was telling the truth. "Well," Regina said, "Those secrets would be all the safer if they were buried… with you six feet under."

Electra smirked, "Well, I have a little arrangement with one of our mutual friends that if anything should happen to me, those secrets will be aired to the public."

I stared at her, and I swallowed.

"Regina."

Regina didn't look at me, and her hand tightened on the dagger's handle "She's bluffing."

"What if she isn't?" Her green eyes peered at me through the darkness, and for a long moment, she was silent. The knife dropped to her side.

"You shan't be trying to murder us anymore, I trust," I said.

Electra leapt to her feet. "Of course not." And we all shook on it, except for Nicholas, who scowled.

Electra made to walk away, 'You know it occurs to me you three haven't figured out how I moved the body. I was with you the whole time after all."

She winked and walked away.

Chapter Forty

Wednesday
14th February, 2024

The worst thing about catching a killer on Monday and not being able to tell anyone about it is that one is required to go to school the next day. Regina and I had to pay a visit to the night nurse as the cuts to our arms were rather deep. Nurse Robin had several questions, and we made up a story about a midnight stroll which ended with us falling down a rocky cliff face.

We had practice in the morning, and of course, we began with a warm-up by running on the beach. Duffy complained about it as always, and I told him, to his bewilderment, "Chin up. You never know when it could save your life."

We had the big game coming up next week, which is, of course, the first game of the season and for Duffy, Archie, James, Gideon, Sidd, Thaddeus, Alexei, Arjun, Windsor, Kipling and me, it would be our first game at the academy. There was a great deal of excitement as everyone's parents would be coming.

"What the sweet hell happened to your arm, Hamlet?" Archie asked as I took off my sweater. I merely regurgitated the same cock and bull story we fed to the nurse.

Archie nodded, "Oh."

"Must have been very sharp rocks," Duffy said.

I nodded, "Oh, they were. Now come on. Game next week and all that," and I jogged back onto the field before I could be questioned further.

After practice, there was a sort of club fair in the great hall. Colin and I went together, and some of the options did sound quite interesting: sea swimming, tiddlywinks, FIFA club, ghost hunting and an Indian students club. As my grandmother is from India, I was rather interested.

Between us, we signed up for 22 clubs. "You know, Colin, you're one of my favourite people, and—"

"Aw, Hamster," he said, slapping his chest, "Going to make my heart burst."

I tried to tackle him onto the grass but failed, and he easily tossed me into the grass. He dropped on the grass and leaned back, smiling up at the clouds, "You know you're right, Hamster, I'd rather spend time with you than anyone else."

I stared at him with the sun and wind in his hair, "Well, you and Emma," he said with a big, goofy grin, "Emma Darjeeling?" I asked, "Isn't she at the prep?"

"Well," he said, "We're dating. We've been texting nonstop. You know she wants to join the polo team next year. I told her to talk to you. I hope you two can be friends. That would be awesome."

"Oh." I said, "Yes, well. I'll tell her all about polo."

We sat in silence for a few moments before he spoke up, "You know we never did finish the third Hobbit movie."

Back in the dorm, Nicholas ended up watching the movie with us, and he had a rather long commentary about the many things they had changed from the books. And then it came out that he had never seen the original trilogy.

Colin gasped, "Now forget about murder, Barking, *that* is a capital offence. Fortunately, one that can be rectified."

Nicholas frowned, "Now I don't see what the big deal is. I read the book. I already know the ending, besides, didn't you two watch the movie recently?" but Colin shushed him.

After Colin fell asleep, Nicholas and I went to brush our teeth. I had forgotten my slippers, and the bathroom floor was cold under my feet. As always, the window was open, and the bathroom smelled most unfortunate. It is almost as if a deodorant factory collapsed into the sewer.

"What are your thoughts on the matter?" I asked as I put my mint toothpaste onto my green toothbrush.

"Well, I am actually quite charmed. Could we watch the second one tomorrow?" he said, "I'm not normally one for adaptations, but the score is simply sublime."

"We certainly can," I said, "But well, I was talking about... You know."

"Ah," he said, "My sister and the deal we cut with her?" He sighed, "I suppose it's for the best. And I do suppose at least this way we can keep an eye on her if nothing else."

I smiled, "Not sure how well I shall sleep knowing that a murderer roams our campus."

"Well, at least during the holidays you get away from the murderer," he said in a whisper, "I don't…and with Mother gone it's just me and her and our father." He was silent for a moment. "What do you think happened to my mother?"

"I don't know." I said, "But we will find out."

He stared at me through the mirror, "How?"

I shrugged, putting my toothpaste and toothbrush back into my pouch, which is green, of course and has the rook crest. "Well, we solved one murder," I said, "How hard can it be to solve another?"

He almost smiled, "Well, when we confront the next murderer, perhaps we ought to be armed and wear chainmail. How's that arm feeling, by the way?"

I frowned at it, "It smarts a little when I move it too much, and it does make playing polo uncomfortable…well, it's not the only thing."

He chuckled. I said, "That encounter with your sister has taught me one thing."

"What might that be?"

"I need to hit the gym," I said. "She almost overpowered us. Can't let that happen again."

He rolled his eyes and ruffled my hair, "Perhaps we ought to join the boxing team."

"Could you imagine Regina in boxing gloves?" I said, and he laughed, "She shall be beautiful and terrible like a ginger Valkyrie."

We fell into silence for a moment, and he watched the dancing trees outside. He frowned and said, "Why did that branch fall? It was a sturdy branch. There was no wind. And it fell just at the right moment!"

I stared at my face in the mirror. I was starting to get acne. "Well… perhaps it was a coincidence, or perhaps there are more things in heaven or earth than dreamed of."

"You're joking", he said, "There must be a rational answer."

"Do you have one?"

"Perhaps it was a weak branch, or a bird, or a rat or something. I don't know," he said.

"Did you see the size of that tree?" I said, "That branch was the size of my leg!"

"Well, it must have been old... or something. There must be a rational explanation for what happened," he said.

"Must there be?"

"What do you mean to say?" He demanded.

I swallowed, "My late aunt, Dahlia, wrote about things in her diary... strange things, old things."

His face had gone slightly pale. "Dahlia Rook… the one who disappeared? What kind of things?"

"Well," I said, taking out my dental floss, which I don't actually use, but I wanted my hands to be busy, "She talked about a man in the trees who talked to her. She was friends with your mother, you know, and with David Monroe."

Nicholas' jaw was flexing, "Do you remember when we were in kindergarten and went to Old Bridge Park, and it was a hot summer's day, and someone got a nosebleed? We found a clearing with an old tree—" At that moment Duffy walked into the washroom, "Hey lads… still up?" he said.

"Oh yes," I said, putting my mouthwash away, "Colin and I were introducing Nicholas to the Lord of the Rings."

Duffy nodded, "Oh nice… I need to pee." Which he proceeded to do very loudly.

Nicholas and I returned to our dorm room, and he chuckled, "I guess Sir Hugh's class is working out as he planned."

I laughed, "We can't let him know.

Chapter Forty-One

Saturday
17th February, 2024

Not very much happened on Friday. Practice was a little more intense with the coming game, and Jago gave us a very rousing speech. In history, we had a boys vs girls debate, and Regina and I had to get our bandages changed by the nurse. Today I slept in a little, and then Regina and I walked over to Headmistress Keyne's cabin. We get a lot of rain here on the island, but today must have been simply record-breaking. A storm came in from the sea, screaming against the windows and tangling the tree tops, and it rained heavily to the point that the fields were all flooded and everyone got rather soaked. Taking the hint, everyone decided to spend the rest of the day indoors.

Lady Keyne ushered us inside with warm words and set our jackets to dry on the fire grate.

She poured out cups of piping hot, well-brewed tea, with milk and plenty of sugar. Jago and Sarah joined us, and we talked about football and the upcoming match. Outside, the rain poured, and the thunder boomed as Lady Keyne busied herself over the stove.

Regina and Sarah then moved on to the subject of field hockey. And that had got Delilah reminiscing about her days at school, when she had been on the team herself. She brought several photo albums, and we pored over them together as we sat on her lavender-patterned sofa.

They were mostly pictures of her, Dahlia and David. I had never seen pictures of Dahlia before, and so it was quite fascinating. She seemed a lively, happy woman with subtle green eyes and long black hair. That painting in the hallway didn't do her justice. And David was a handsome, smiling chap, so much so that it was rather hard connecting him with the bitter man I had met. It must have been rather hard for Delilah; one best friend gone, and the other gone round the bend.

Jago asked, "How is that tea?"

"Oh, I quite like it," I said, "Just the thing for this sort of weather."

"You know," he said, "There are orcas around here...we should try and spot a few, sometime."

"Oh, how that's lovely," I said, "we simply must. Oh, did you know that orcas are actually dolphins? Oh yes, their name, killer whale, actually started off as whale killer. Isn't that fascinating?"

One of the pictures was of Dahlia and Delilah standing knee deep in the surf, the sky was grey and the sea as well. Their hair was caught up in the wind, and their smiles were wide. Delilah had been holding a hurricane lamp.

"What's happening here?" I asked, pointing at the picture

She stopped in the middle of showing Regina a picture of her old hockey uniform. She frowned a little at the old picture, "Oh, we were just being silly. Dahlia had a book in the library... *Ways of the Old World* or something like that, and we were trying out something she'd read."

Regina said, "Oh, because spirits are blown in by a storm? Granny always told me that. That's why one always must always close their windows during a storm."

Sarah said, "Oh. These old wives' tales are ever so quaint."

Delilah smiled, "Well, dear, some of them are more than old wives' tales."

Before I could answer, Jago leaned over, "Oh well, it does look quite fun," he said. His mother closed the album, "It was just nonsense. Some things shouldn't be messed with."

"Did it work?" Regina asked, "Did anything happen?"

"No, nothing at all. Nothing happened. We were just being silly."

There was a moment of silence, interrupted when a clap of thunder growled at the windowpanes. She sighed, "Looks like that storm is getting worse. Jago, would you be so kind as to walk these two back to the towers, and Sarah back to her own dorm?" Jago nodded, jumping up, "Certainly."

Delilah bid us goodbye and told us we were welcome back anytime. Outside, the rain had stopped, but the sky was swollen and bruised and threatened further rain. We walked Sarah back to her dorm, and she went inside with a wave and 'Cheerio'.

Once she was gone, Jago smiled, "You know, at some point we really must give it a try."

Regina nodded. "Certainly, Keyne, but today Hamlet and I have plans." Leaving Jajo, we headed to the library to retrieve 'Ways of the Old World' from the library.

Back in the dorm, the others were watching a movie in the common room, and we joined them once we'd showered and dried ourselves off. Fiona and Polly were curled up together on a chair, Duffy sat at their feet, and Fiona was braiding his hair. Archie sat on his own in one of the armchairs and was chatting with Nicholas. Others hung around the common room in groups or alone. Colin wasn't there.

Polly smiled at us as we dropped into the empty armchairs, "And how was tea with Headmistress Keyne?"

"Oh, very lovely," Regina answered, "She's an excellent hostess and makes a good cup."

Fiona hummed, "Oh and Hamlet, darling, you left a message for you."

I frowned, "You?"

"Oh no, darling," she said, "Sir Hugh left a message for you. He said that he's at a conference next week. and so you shan't be having detention all of next week."

Regina's gaze was on me, "Oh, that's good news, isn't it, darling?"

The others all hung out in the common room watching movie after movie, which included a back-to-back *Barbie* and *Oppenheimer*. Nicholas rather liked both.

Meanwhile, I had started to read the book. It was quite a ponderous, old thing that added quite a lot of weight to my already heavy bag. It was quite yellowed, but when I opened the cover, it opened smoothly. I skipped past the introductions and the blah blah, and I flipped through the various chapters, which included a very long treatise on the beliefs of the early man, the magic in the cycle of the seasons, spirit flight, and stuff like that. I noticed then something scribbled on the top of one of the pages, the crest of the Lord and Lady Greenwood, roughly drawn and vague, but it was that crest.

I looked up at the others, all deeply engrossed in their documentary. I cleared my throat, feeling sorry for interrupting, but I couldn't help myself. "Do any of you know a Lord and Lady Greenwood?"

Regina's eyes met mine, and Nicholas was looking over at me, too. "No," Archie said, "Why do you ask?"

Regina rose from her seat and sauntered over to me, peering down on the pages in front of us, "My, my," she said, "Our mysterious friends do have a habit of popping up everywhere, don't they?"

I looked at her, "Oh yes, they do!"

Chapter Forty-Two

Saturday morning
24th February, 2024

Well, once again, Regina De Winter had blown my whole world apart.

All week I spent waiting for the big game against St Abernathy, and so much of the week was spent either at practice or thinking about practice. The game was everything I had dreamed of. All our parents had come and were in the stands. I was as nervous as a cat. Jago gave a rather rousing speech, which I am fairly certain he pilfered from Game of Thrones, but it was a very good speech. As we ran out onto the field, the cheers were deafening, and it all fell silent for the kick-off. And the game began.

We, Saint Bart's, boys played like a well-oiled machine, and certainly the Abernathy lot made a most valiant effort, but we wiped the pitch with them. And as we won 5-nil, I say that with little exaggeration. I scored the last goal, and then I got happily crushed by the rather jubilant team in the world's biggest group hug.

There were lots of handshakes and lots of people ruffled my hair, but then Sir Hugh called out for us to "exercise good sportsmanship," and so we lined up to shake the Abernathy's kids' hands and tell them 'good game', which was a lie, but I suppose some lies are necessary in this polite, curious world we live in.

Then we walked out of the pitch. Sir Hugh clapped me on the shoulder, "Well played, Lord Hamlet. I am proud of you," he said, "You know, in *King Lear,* which is by far one of my favourite plays…"

"That's quite all right, Sir, thank you," I chuckled.

He laughed, "Oh, just as well, I am not entirely sure what point I was making. The bard wasn't making a favourable comparison. He does refer to the sport as 'base'. But in his day, football wasn't the beautiful sport it is today. It was quite deadly, really. In fact, more people died playing football than sword fighting. It was quite a vulgar game back then and…"

Mercifully, Lord Barking and Mother strolled over together, and Lord Barking clapped Hugh on the back, "Oh come, Hugh, can't have you boring the poor boy to death, especially today."

"Oh, actually, Harry, young Hamlet has become something of a Shakespearean these past few weeks," Sir Hugh said.

"Oh, really?" Mother said, "Miracles do happen, I suppose."

Lord Barking clapped me on the back, "You were excellent out there. I am proud of you, son."

"Thank you, Lord Barking," I said.

At that point, Nicholas and Regina had strolled over together. Regina beamingly gave the other a kiss on the cheek and shook Lord Barking… Harry's hand.

Nicholas, with a stony face, said, "Father, My Lady."

Lord Barking stared at his son for a long moment, but Mother smiled warmly, "And how has your term been going, Nicholas?"

Nicholas stuttered on the verge of speech for a moment but managed, "Well… I think Hamlet described it best as 'quite eventful,' and yes, it certainly had been that."

Sir Hugh beamed, "Oh yes, as inexplicable as it is, I must say that the pair of them have become quite good friends. I suppose you're right, Isohel, miracles do happen."

"Murder makes for odd bedfellows," Regina said, "You know, Your Grace, when we parted ways in London, Hamlet promised that he would give you the identity of the true murderer. And now if the six of us could find a quiet place to talk, all shall be revealed."

Sir Hugh had fallen silent, and Mother looked confused, but Lord Harry nodded, "Certainly. Hugh, might we make use of your office?"

Once inside, Regina waited until the three were seated to begin. She cleared her throat, "Well, first of all and as I am sure you all know, poor Sarah Smith was actually Miss Jenny Leach, a private detective hired by the late, lamented Lady Barking. So there you go, you have your traitor."

There was no surprise on any of their faces, and Regina went on, "Well, now for the person who pushed poor Miss Leach out the window. That person was..." And she gestured to Nicholas, who said, "It was Electra, Dad, it was Electra. Hamlet figured it out."

Lord Barking had gone quite pale, "Electra?" he whispered.

"Oh yes," I went on, "She was quite daring. Stole Nicky's cufflink, hid in Miss Leach's room, waited till she was alone, pushed her out the window and climbed down herself and then the night proceeded."

Lord Barking was showing signs of wanting to speak, but Regina silenced him with a finger, "Now you'll notice I referred to Electra as 'the person who pushed Poor Miss Leach out the window' and not as 'the person who killed poor Miss Leach.'

And that is because they are two very different people."

I stared in shocked silence, and so did Nicholas. Everyone in the room was staring at her in rapt attention. Regina De Winter always did have everyone wrapped around her finger. And she went on, "You see, Miss Leach had started a phone call in the moments before Electra attacked, and the following morning Hamlet and I found her phone still working. You know, one thing about Second Eden phones: they are quite sturdy, capable of surviving a three-foot drop and then a night in freezing temperatures. But the call went to voicemail and upon listening to it I realised that after she landed, Miss Leach had been alive for quite some time."

"What?" I demanded, and she shushed me and went on.

"I sent the voice note to myself before I turned in the phone, and upon closer inspection, one can hear Hammy discovering her, you can hear Baskerville barking, and then you can hear a woman's voice saying 'so you' or that's what I thought she'd been saying."

She paused for a moment for dramatic effect, "But you know I have come to realise that in English words can sound so much alike, hare, h-a-r-e can sound like hair h-a-i-r, for instance and 'so you' can sound like 'Sir Hugh.'" I turned to Sir Hugh, and he was silent and made no denial.

"When we confronted Electra," Regina went on, "She walked away quite smug that for all we had figured out, we hadn't figured out how she moved the body. And she was right. Well, now we know, she must have come into the house and told Sir what happened. After all, we were all told that no matter what problems we might have, we could trust Sir Hugh. And Electra did just that, and of course. She must have gone to him, told him what happened. Sir Hugh found that woman, and drove her off and left her to die in the snow… what was it David Monroe said about you cleaning up?"

Sir Hugh finally spoke, "Well. And I won't beat about the bush. Yes, Electra Barking came to me; she told me all about her brother's spy and that she'd killed her. She told me where I could find that woman, and so I did. I picked her up, and I drove her away from the manor grounds. I drove away from the moor, away from Great Sacrifice and far away from the Rook name. I drove at night, left her near the town and returned. I have protected our family before, My Lady, and I will do it again."

Mother stared at me, "I did say Sir Hugh is a father to us, and I meant it."

She placed a hand on his shoulder.

Lord Barking, with a smile that didn't reach his eyes, "Well. Hamlet and Regina, I do suppose you delivered. Hugh, next time one of my children kills someone… or attempts to, I would appreciate it if you tell me so I don't punish the wrong one."

Nicholas spoke for the first time, "Yes… You knew it was Electra, and you let me take the fall for it. You let him drag me back to that house… why?" Regina squeezed his shoulder.

Sir Hugh looked horrified with himself, "I am sorry, Lord Nicholas, but when I realised your father suspected you, I did urge your sister to confess, but your sister has certain evidence she obtained from Jenny Leach after she attacked her. What she said would destroy many, should it ever get out. I couldn't let that happen, and I am truly sorry."

Nicholas clenched his fist and hung his head, and I realised he was crying, "You tried to tell me," I said, "when I came to your office to sign the permission slip – love, hatred, and greed," I echoed, and he nodded. Regina smiled, "Well, I suppose it all did work out for the best. And now we'll give you all that information to deal with as you please," she said with a curtsy, "My Lord, My Lady, Headmaster."

Chapter Forty-Three

I realised the parcel David had given me was still in it. My curiosity burned as I tore open the parcel, revealing a small, green-bound book. A diary. The spine was worn, the cover scuffed with age. When I flipped it open, my confusion only deepened. Written in faded ink on the inside cover, in an elegant, looping hand, I did not know was a name I did know – *The Diary of Dahlia Rook.*

The pages were filled, cover to cover, with delicate script, thoughts and memories carefully preserved in ink. It was almost uncanny, a long-dead woman whose voice and memory were resurrected from the past, whispered through words almost like a ghost. But it was what I found tucked into the back of the diary that made my pulse quicken. Yellowed newspaper clippings, pressed between the final pages like dried flowers.

Ambassador Southron's Daughter Found Dead in London.
Chelsea Man Slain in Brutal Stabbing.
Woman Found Drowned in the Thames.
Lord Patel's Heir Dead in a Fire.
Wicklow Victim Linked to Gravedigger.

The headlines sprawled before me, disjointed yet eerily methodical. I read them all, scanning dates, places – different days, different cities, even different countries. Some were murders, some accidents, and others suicides. No clear connection. No common thread.

Except, of course, that my aunt had kept them.

I ran my fingers over the brittle edges, my mind racing. She had gathered these names, these tragedies, and preserved them as though they *meant* something.

I closed the book, my heartbeat loud in my ears. Apparently, my aunt had a taste for the macabre.

I felt an odd shudder as I lifted the leather cover. And the spine... the book's spine... cracked like old wood in a forest. I don't know how it got there. I had never seen this damned book before in my life, and I certainly hadn't packed it.

I rifled through the pages again, scanning the neat, slanted script, when something slipped free and fluttered to the floor. A piece of glossy cardstock. An invitation.

> *Lord and Lady Greenwood request your presence at the garden party this summer. 20th July, 2000. Details of the location to follow.*

The lettering was embossed in deep green, elegant and precise. And there, pressed into the corner in wax, was the face.

That face.

A Green Man, grinning with leaves for lips and ivy-threaded eyes. The same face that had been on the envelope that had come with those damned flowers. Greenwood. And so I did what I always do, and told Regina.

"Well, darlings," she said to the others one day during breakfast in a slightly grave tone. "We do have something else to tell you, so today after biology, hang back in the classroom, and we can have a nice private chat."

Biology on Fridays was our last class of the day, so it was perfect. Biology was my favourite class and the one I did best in, though I did well in all my classes. Anyway, once the lesson had finished and Professor Grey and the other students had filed out, Regina had locked the door and drawn down the shade.

I put down the frog skeleton I had been admiring and walked over, opening up Dahlia's diary and pressing it onto the table. I said, "This is my Aunt Dahlia's diary. She was at school at the same time as Mother, Lady Moira, Lord Harry, David Monroe, Headmistress Keyne, and many other people."

They all nodded, slightly confused. "She had in her diary several newspaper clippings," I said, fanning them out on the table. "Some were strangers, people attacked or people who took their own lives.

But some of these deaths were people known to us, or I suppose people whose relatives we know."

I slid the article about Lord Patel's heir over to Archie, "This was Sidd's uncle. He went to school here. He died in a seemingly accidental fire." I picked up another, "This was Lucy Southron. She, too, went here and was stabbed four times in London."

"Oh, yes," Fiona said, taking a clip from me, "My dad and Nigel Southron are great friends. It was quite a tragedy, apparently."

I nodded, "All of these seem unconnected – some suicides, some murders, some accidents." They looked at the articles, passing them around and whispering about them. Regina cleared her throat, "Well, and there's more. Hamlet and I have noticed a trend. Several of these are men and women who drowned themselves in the Thames. And as you all remember, Hamlet and I did find the body of a woman stabbed in the park."

"And what's more," I said, taking out a bundle of paper, "These are all about the Gravedigger. I looked at some of the victims, and again, at least some of them were relatives of people we know; there was Melissa Kipling, Vanessa Willoughby-Sage, and—"

"And my uncle," Polly said, "Peter Shrewsbury."

There was silence for a few minutes before Colin spoke up, "I am quite confused. What are you suggesting, Hammy?

"I think in some way these deaths are all connected, and I think my aunt thought so too," I said, "That's why she saved all of these articles. I know that's quite out there, but here me out, please hear me out."

They all fell into grave silence, and I went on, "My aunt and Lady Moira were friends. They were also friends with David Monroe and Headmistress Keyne. I think that they were investigating the Gravedigger, and that he or she was someone in our world. I think they got too close, and that got my aunt killed."

"Now, I know," I went on, "And what's more… the four of them…" I said stuttering. I struggled for a moment with words, but Regina stepped in, "They were all witches. Now, darlings, I know that's quite a heavy pill to swallow, but swallow it you must."

There was silence for a very long moment, and I broke it, "Well, I think Moira Barking was murdered. I think my aunt was, too. And all these others too," I said, "I think in some way their deaths were connected. They have to be. And I think part of the key to all this is David Monroe. It was he who told Nicholas after the funeral that he should hire that woman."

Regina nodded, "Well now, my darlings," she said, "I know what this all seems rather out there. But there is a connection."

The four of them were silent for a moment, and Duffy spoke up, "Well then, I daresay we'd best start investigating. We do have a killer to catch." And there was a resounding sound of agreement.

We all parted ways after all of us running back to our dorms or whatever, they all had a lot to digest, and any investigation or whatnot could wait. Nicholas had picked up his book as soon as we got back to our dorm, and I watched him lose himself in elves and dark lords for a while before I sat next to him.

"Well, I know that summer is ages away, but what are your plans?" I asked, "I must confess I am rather worried about you all cooped up with your sister all summer."

He shrugged, "Oh well, what can one do about it? Besides, worry not, Rook, I plan on locking myself in my room with a large pile of books. I shall be completely undisturbed, and to be honest, I can think of no better way to spend the summer."

I looked up at his pale, elegant face, "Is that really how you want to spend a summer? Reading?"

His smile was thin and pale. "You know, Rook, it's quite odd… all the things that used to bring me joy; reading, writing, poetry… tormenting you… they don't… I don't… I don't know how to describe it," Nicholas said. "I just feel empty inside, like there is a hollow where I used to be, and I don't know how to fill it."

I was silent for a long moment, "Well, you don't have to do it at your place. Rook library has an excellent pile of books, you know. Some of them are quite old, and if I recall, we have some rather rare books," I said.

"Are you inviting me over the summer, Rook?" he asked, almost sounding incredulous. "Well, if you are genuine, I must say I am enticed."

"Well, excellent,' I said, "But as for you being undisturbed. I can't promise that. I do expect you to be somewhat social. And I shall insist on our going on at least one walk a day. I can't have you wasting an entire summer indoors."

"Oh, of course not,' I said, "Just the Darlings."

He made a humph sound, "Hm, alright, alright, just them. But I still expect to spend most of my time locked up in the library."

"Of course," I said, "But don't forget. We do have a murderer to catch."

He nodded, "It seems I have quite a busy summer ahead of me – solving a murder, reading books. It does sound ideal."

"So, shall I take that as a yes?"

Nicholas smiled, "You know what they say... to the Rooky Wood and all that."

* * *